The Enchanted World

MAGICAL BEASTS

The Enchanted World

MAGICAL BEASTS

by the Editors of Time-Life Books

The Content

Time-Life Books · Amsterdam

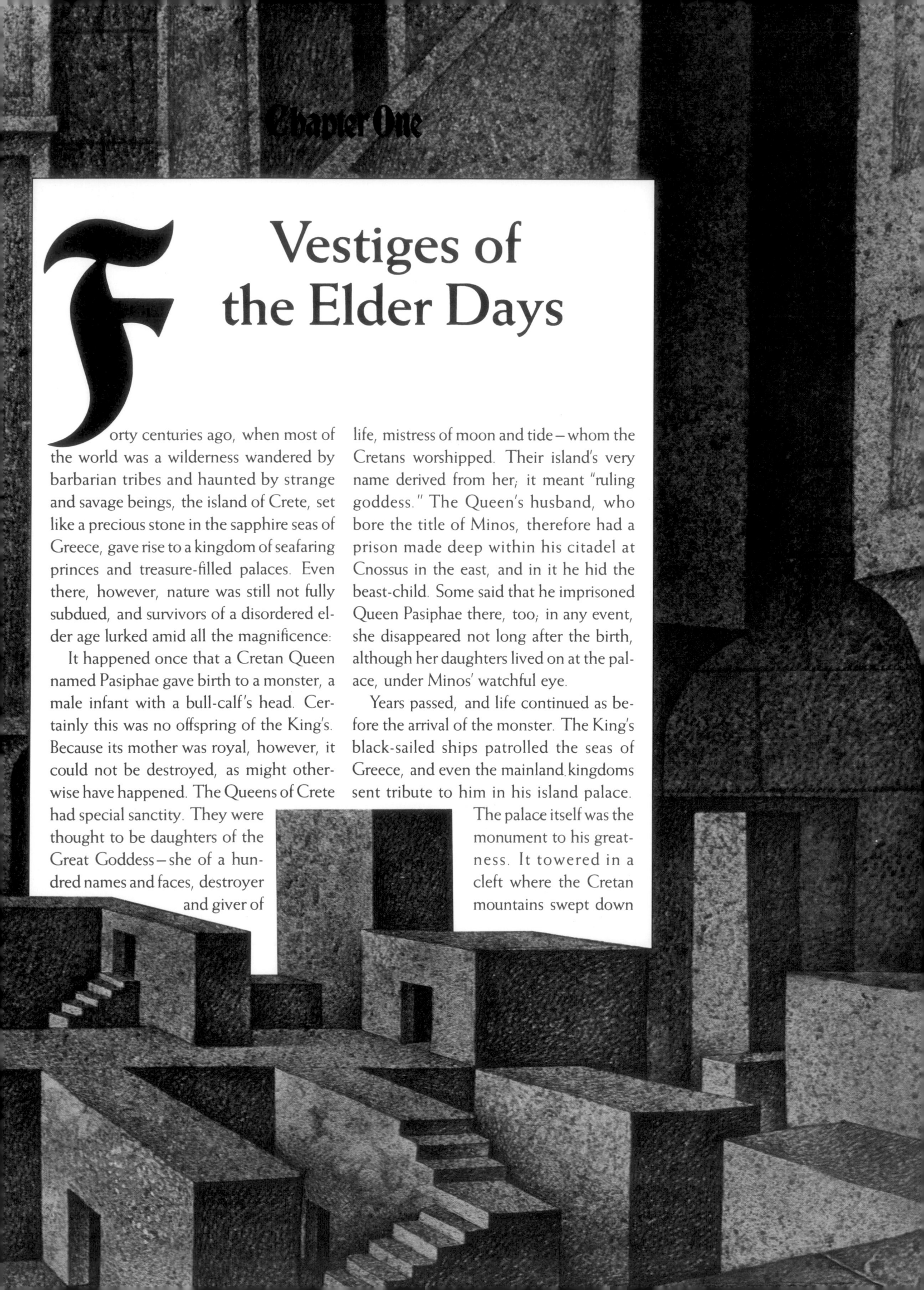

Chapter One

Vestiges of the Elder Days

Forty centuries ago, when most of the world was a wilderness wandered by barbarian tribes and haunted by strange and savage beings, the island of Crete, set like a precious stone in the sapphire seas of Greece, gave rise to a kingdom of seafaring princes and treasure-filled palaces. Even there, however, nature was still not fully subdued, and survivors of a disordered elder age lurked amid all the magnificence:

It happened once that a Cretan Queen named Pasiphae gave birth to a monster, a male infant with a bull-calf's head. Certainly this was no offspring of the King's. Because its mother was royal, however, it could not be destroyed, as might otherwise have happened. The Queens of Crete had special sanctity. They were thought to be daughters of the Great Goddess—she of a hundred names and faces, destroyer and giver of life, mistress of moon and tide—whom the Cretans worshipped. Their island's very name derived from her; it meant "ruling goddess." The Queen's husband, who bore the title of Minos, therefore had a prison made deep within his citadel at Cnossus in the east, and in it he hid the beast-child. Some said that he imprisoned Queen Pasiphae there, too; in any event, she disappeared not long after the birth, although her daughters lived on at the palace, under Minos' watchful eye.

Years passed, and life continued as before the arrival of the monster. The King's black-sailed ships patrolled the seas of Greece, and even the mainland kingdoms sent tribute to him in his island palace. The palace itself was the monument to his greatness. It towered in a cleft where the Cretan mountains swept down to the sea, and it was unfortified: Minos, ruler of the seas, had no need of protective walls. Instead, tier upon tier of white stone chambers, sunny courtyards, bright pavilions and sweeping stairways served as a stage for the suave and graceful ceremonies of the Cretan court.

Yet there was a sense of hovering darkness, too. Above the tiled roofs and the forests of crimson columns soared a stark stone emblem: the curved horns of an enormous bull, the ancestral animal of the Cretan house. And far from the airy royal chambers where painted dolphins danced in glowing seas and images of lilies gilded the walls, far from the storerooms with their treasures of oil, wine, grain and gold, down along a seldom-visited corridor there was a massive door. From this portal, the beast's prison twisted deep into the earth—miles of lightless corridors that curled and writhed upon themselves to make a fathomless maze.

Within the maze, shuffling aimlessly through its eternal night, lived the monster, which was called the Minotaur, or "Bull of Minos." When it reached its full growth, its massive head was that of a bull, crescent-horned and covered with coarse hair, matted from the spittle that dribbled from its blackened lips into its dewlap. Its body was a human figure, powerfully built, with legs thickened by a lifetime of bearing the burden of its great head.

While the hours and days and years rolled by and the busy life of maritime princes bustled above its cavern, the Minotaur lived a mole's life in darkness and silence. It was always alone. It did not speak; it could not. For the most part, it ate small cave creatures—rats, insects, lizards. It would hear them scuttling and would catch their scent. Then it rumbled in its throat and went hunting.

The Minotaur was always a successful predator. Besides knowing every curve and cranny of its territory, it had something of a man's cunning. It also had great strength, which served for those rare occasions when people entered the maze and it might partake of human flesh.

Such feasts were rare but regular. Since

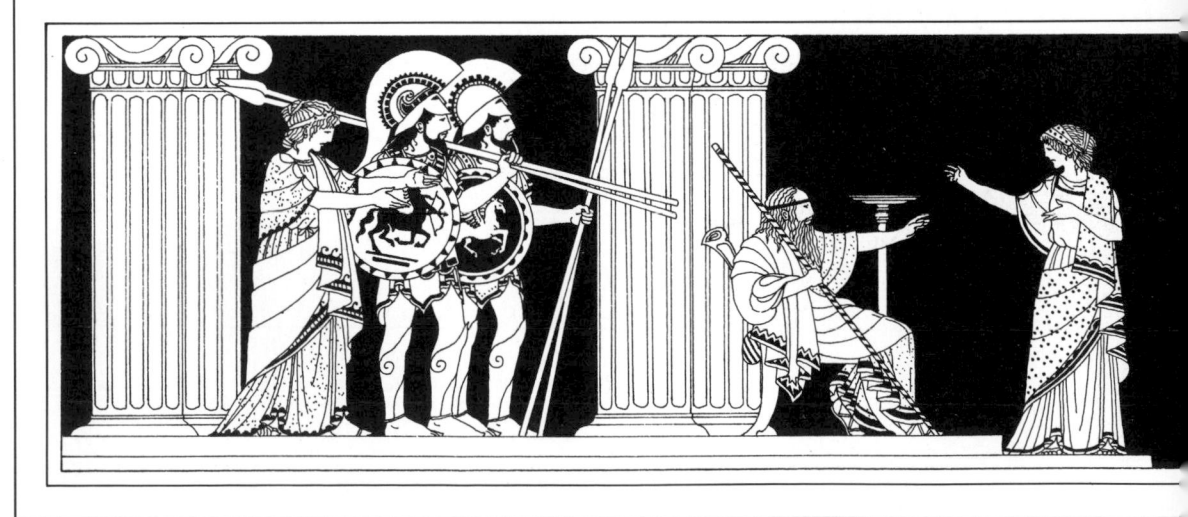

Every nine years, Minos, King of Crete, demanded human sacrifice for his Minotaur, a savage
was ordered to supply the sacred offering. Seven youths and seven maidens were

the earliest days of their civilization, Cretans had offered sacrifices—slaves or captives of war—to their goddess at the turn of the Great Year. This occurred every ninth year; the date was determined by the cycles of the planet Venus when it appeared as the morning star, one of the Great Goddess's many faces. At one time, the victims had been dispatched by the *labrys*, a double-headed ax that was still to be seen in the ritual chambers of Minos' citadel. Now, by order of the King, the Minotaur served as a living ax, and the beast's prison came to be called the Labyrinth.

Within that maze no mortal could last long. Even if the victims kept sufficiently still to avoid rousing the beast, they ultimately starved. One way or another, the Minotaur got the bodies in the end and feasted on the flesh and sucked the marrow from the bones. As long as it did so, the people said, the Cretan ships remained full-sailed, the groves heavy-laden and the granaries overflowing.

And so it happened during the spring of a certain year, when the chill rains had ceased and Venus sparkled in the rosy dawns, that Crete began preparing for the festival of the sacrifice. The fields were plowed, and the black earth lay warming in the sun, ready for the seed. In the olive groves, small, cunningly jointed dolls—hopeful offerings for the Great Goddess—hung among the boughs and jigged like living things with each breath of wind. In a palace courtyard, the King's daughter Ariadne turned gravely on a mosaic dancing floor, whose decoration guided the convoluted steps of her ritual dance; the floor itself was patterned after the brushwood mazes used for trapping the partridges that the dance was named for. In a chamber frescoed with griffins, Minos gave orders and waited for word that the victims had arrived. And in the depths of the Labyrinth, the Minotaur wandered.

The sacrificial victims came one April day by water from Athens. Seven youths and seven maidens had been promised—chosen by lot to serve as tribute to Minos from that half-barbarian kingdom in Attica, on the mainland. All of the palace people went down to the quay at the port of Cnossus to greet them, as was the custom.

creature, half-man, half-bull. One year, the city-state of Athens, which owed fealty to Crete, chosen by lot. Then all the elders of Athens wept as the victims were taken away.

Brown-haired Ariadne stood there on the stones, among the palace priestesses in their tiered skirts and snaking arm bands; Minos waited near her, surrounded by the young men of his court. Around them surged a chattering crowd of sailors and merchants, galley slaves and palace servants. All fell silent when the ship came into view, gliding past the little island of Dia, far out on a sun-burnished sea.

The ship's black sail was furled, and a canopy hid the captives on the deck. Her thirty oars glittered, rising and falling to the beat of a drum that sounded clearly across the water. As the ship neared land, the oars snapped upright, motionless as rows of ebony spears, and the vessel slid in to dock. But before she could be secured, a man from among the group of sacrificial victims shouldered past the guards and oarsmen and leaped onto the quay.

He was thickset and heavily muscled; his hair was black, and his blue eyes shone out from a scarred thug's face. He scanned the crowd until he spotted Minos, who wore a plumed crown. Without hesitation, the young man strode to the King.

"I am Theseus, son of the King of Athens, and I have been chosen for sacrifice," he said coolly. "Until we go to the death, the children of Athens are in my care."

The priestesses twittered, the courtiers stirred. Theseus was already famous in popular songs as an adventurer and an intrepid fighter; it was said that he had invented the art of wrestling and that he had—barehanded—killed a fire-breathing bull, sent to Athens from Minos' own sacred herd. His exploits and strength had led to rumors that his father was not Aegeus, the King of Athens, but Poseidon, the sea-god. Here was a challenger rather than a despairing victim. The orderly ceremony had been disturbed.

Minos, however, was used to command and to action. Accounts differed as to what happened next. Some said that he declared his own divine ancestry, scoffed at the possibility that Theseus was fathered by the sea-god, and set the Athenian a test to prove it. Others recorded that he simply silenced the crowd and went on with the ceremony.

In any event, the ritual provided The-

the young Athenians were mourned as though they had already met their
Theseus, son of the King of Athens, and a warrior without peer.

seus with an opportunity to demonstrate his prowess. The Kings of Crete—whose title, Minos, meant "Moon Being"—were thought to wed the sea with a ring each Great Year, for the moon and the sea were as closely linked as lovers. Accordingly, Minos now drew from his hand a signet— not one of the ceramic wrist medallions that most Cretans wore, but a heavy ring of twisted gold—and tossed it into the harbor. Before the ring had disappeared, Theseus dived into the water after it, piercing the surface like a living arrow.

For a moment nothing happened. Then a dolphin leaped into the air, clutching something golden in its mouth and shaking its sleek head in triumph. It disappeared, and an instant later, Theseus' head broke the surface at that very spot. He swam easily to the quay, climbed onto the stones and raised both arms before the crowd. In one hand, he clasped Minos' great ring. In the other, he held a crown—a circlet of gold leaves hung with ruby roses.

"My prizes from the sea, Minos," said the Athenian. "A ring from a mighty king and a crown from the depths."

But Minos sustained his majestic calm. He signaled that the ritual should go on, and guards led Theseus and his companions up the long road toward the palace. Ignoring the procession, Minos turned to observe his daughter Ariadne. She was staring after Theseus.

That night, the ceremonies proceeded in their stately pace. The fourteen victims were feasted in the palace, a last meal for those who would soon be fodder. The children of Athens said little—all except Theseus, that is. He strolled easily among the courtiers, a wine cup always in his hand. And because he was a king's son and a brave adventurer who was soon to meet a cruel death, the Cretans gathered around him, curious and pitying. Even Ariadne, momentarily escaping the stern eyes of Minos, drew close to hear him speak. Theseus smiled upon her when she approached. He had a charming smile, and he had seen her watching him when he emerged from the sea.

In the warren of chambers and corridors

In the maze of the Cretan Labyrinth, deep beneath the palace of King Minos,
Theseus slew the Minotaur. Besides his own great strength, the youth had
weapons to aid him, secretly supplied by Minos' daughter Ariadne.

and corners that formed the palace of Cnossus, secret assignations, even with prisoners, were not hard to bring about, especially when the woman was the daughter of the Queen. Sometime that night, while the palace slept, Ariadne met Theseus alone. He left that meeting with the weapons that might save him; she left with a promise that he gave most sweetly.

In the morning, before sunlight had slanted into the deepest of the palace courtyards, Theseus and his Athenian companions were taken to the door that led to the Labyrinth and the Minotaur. They stood in a grim group, while Minos intoned prayers and the priestesses wailed and chanted. At length and quite abruptly, the door was swung open and the Athenians were pushed into the gloom. A single torch was handed to them to provide light. Then the iron bolts crashed home. As the echoes died, the prisoners could hear, outside the door, the priestesses' skirts rustle and clink. The women hurried away. The captain of the guard gave sharp orders, and sandals drummed on the stones. Then all was quiet. One of the Athenian maidens began to weep.

"Make no sound." Theseus said in a low voice. Taking the torch, he instructed the others to stand motionless until he commanded otherwise. Then he flung back his victim's cloak to reveal a short bronze sword and a ball of rough wool. "Gifts from the Cretan Princess," he said. "The wool is full of magic. It will keep me from getting lost in the maze."

He raised the torch a moment to illuminate three archways in the walls ahead, identically empty and black. Then he unrolled a bit of wool, knotted it to a stone protruding from the lintel and let the ball drop. It rolled to the right, hesitated, veered to the left, then, finding its direction, disappeared into the center archway, unwinding as it went. Theseus followed.

Huddled together, the Athenians did as Theseus had told them: Without the torch, they had no choice. The cold air stank of dung and decay. Hardly any sounds issued from the seamless darkness, no more than small rustlings and scuttlings on the stone, whisperings as the wool thread moved or tautened. The sound that each ear listened for — the bellow of the beast — did not come.

Hours passed. Then, between one moment and the next, Theseus was with them

again, invisible in the dark, for he no longer had the torch. He panted, he was soaking wet, and he reeked. Without a word, he pushed his countrymen aside and struck the door three times. It swung open. Ariadne stood in the corridor, a finger at her lips. She blanched when she saw Theseus. Blood was hardening in his hair. His eyelashes were spiky with it, and gore bloomed in scarlet patches on the rags of his robe. He still held the strand of wool in one hand, and the clots on his fingers stuck to it. But he was alive, and nodded in answer to Ariadne's questioning look: The beast was dead. Of how he had found it (or been found) and how he had slain it, he did not say, then or later.

Ariadne contrived to hide the captives that day. And when darkness fell, she led them down the road to the harbor of Cnossus and a galley that waited there.

To succeed in all of this was a remarkable feat for a young woman, especially one sheltered and coddled in the palace of Minos. But she was the descendant of mighty queens, and she loved Theseus. He took her onto the ship and, in an absent-minded way, let her sit in the bow with him. He had promised to make her his queen. Indeed, he gave her the golden crown he had rescued from the sea. No one ever knew what became of Minos' ring.

Oars creaking, water hissing under the bow, the galley sped across the darkling sea with its scattered, peaked islands — little Dia, pine-covered Thera and brown Ios — and into the strait between Paros and Naxos, where the scent of wild thyme drifted out across the water. At Naxos, the ship grated up onto the shingle, and the

Satyrs—cheerful goat-men who haunted the island glades of Greece—had a limitless desire for
mortal women. It was the satyrs, storytellers said, who rescued the Cretan Princess
Ariadne when her Athenian lover Theseus left her sleeping on the shores of Naxos.

Athenians bathed and rested. When dusk fell, Theseus sailed away from the island, ghosting across the water as lightly as the night wind. But he left Ariadne behind, sleeping on the shore. A Cretan wife would do him little good in Athens.

Little is known of Ariadne's fate. Some legends say Dionysus, god of the vine, married her and took her to live with him and his tribe of satyrs—goat-footed men—in the leafy Naxian groves. Eventually, it was said, Ariadne was overcome by fear of the Great Goddess's wrath at her betrayal of the ritual, and hanged herself from a tree branch, where her body swung in the breeze much like the dolls that hung in the olive groves of her Cretan home. Her rose-studded crown Dionysus then hurled into the heavens, to glitter forever in the northern summer sky.

As for Theseus, he sailed to the sacred island of Delos to perform rites of thanksgiving. Then, in a leisurely manner, he headed for home.

At the beginning of his venture, Theseus had told his grieving father that if he should return alive and victorious over the Minotaur, he would change the Cretans' black sail for a white one; this would be the sign for Aegeus to rejoice. But the ship that bore down upon the Attic shore carried a black sail. Theseus had neglected to make the change. (Tactful chroniclers later wrote that some god had put a "strange and cruel forgetfulness" into his mind.) When report of the black-sailed ship was brought to Aegeus, he thought his only son had died. In his sorrow, he flung himself from a promontory into the sea, which thenceforth was known as the Aegean in his honor. Theseus assumed the crown of Athens as its rightful heir.

Once in power, Theseus proved to be a good, strong King. He united the various warring Attic kingdoms under his rule at Athens, and as his power waxed, that of Minos waned. The killing of the sacred man-beast by a mortal seemed to wither the island kingdom. Crete was devastated not once but many times: Earthquake and fire brought the palace down, it was said. Floods drowned the groves and fields. And, at last, invading mainland peoples imposed their rule on what was left of the once-brilliant Cretan civilization.

That such glories could so swiftly and wholly come to ruin was unusual even in those turbulent times. Yet people knew all too well how unpredictable the world and its workings could be. Theseus and Minos lived in a raw age when the earth was replete with mysteries. For the most part, the vast and verdant forests of the planet were uncut, the rolling seas uncharted, the cloud-piercing peaks untrod.

In the wilderness, and even in the settled lands, more beasts than men lived. The beasts existed in bewildering and changeable variety, as if nature itself were confused or had not yet finished the work of creation. Among earth-bound creatures of that time were some with men's bodies and goats' feet, or with men's torsos and horses' bodies. Lambs could be grown on special trees. Among the creatures of the air were winged horses, birds of prey with lions' bodies, birds that cast human shadows, and birds that hatched from barnacles rather than from eggs. And in that era, though rarely seen, lived unicorns—graceful horses adorned with a single, spiraling horn and blessed with the powers of purification and healing.

All of the members of this exuberant flowering of animal forms seemed, like the unicorn, to be imbued with more than mortal powers. Springing as they evidently had from the dawning of the world, they carried in them—for good or evil—something of the potency of the earliest gods. And while they were worshipped, they were also feared by humankind.

Their future was shadowed. As the human family spread and grew in strength, these beasts would disappear or disperse into remote wildernesses, to be seen only by intrepid explorers and become the stuff of travelers' tales. But when the world was in its infancy, humans—who, after all, were animals themselves—shared it easily with a host of other animals and with beings whose natures were both human and not human. The mortals were not masters then. Puny latecomers to the planet, they bowed down to the powers of the wild and paid the animals honor.

many generations before the ancestors of Minos and Theseus learned to plow and sow and harvest, humans lived by hunting and gathering. In small bands, these early people ranged across a Europe that embraced great tracts of tundra—wind-swept terrain covered with lichens, mosses and hardy grasses, and studded only occasionally with stands of birch and alder. Theirs was a bitterly cold world, chilled by enormous ice sheets that grew in the snowy mountains and pushed outward with irresistible force. But it was a rich world for hunting. Herds of mammoths, woolly rhinoceroses, long-horned aurochs, bison and other grazing beasts roamed the land. And there were other, more dangerous animals as well—massive lions, saber-toothed cats and, most fearsome of all, the cave bear, a fierce, strong beast nine feet high.

To these early hunters, the cave bear had sovereign status, ruling over all other animals. Humans paid the Animal Master obeisance believing that his favor brought them prey: In return for human veneration, he allowed some of his subjects to be slain by the hunters' spears. If they failed to honor him, they would starve.

In later days, many of the Ice Age grazing animals and predators died out, and the Animal Master himself disappeared. Perhaps this was due to the warming of the climate; perhaps, too, humans played a role. Alien peoples were swarming into Europe during those distant millennia, and their hunting skills were great. If they venerated other gods, they may have slain the cave bear. Ultimately, all that remained to suggest the Master's former status were graves created by the earlier hunters: When the bears had died of natural causes in their grottoes, the human worshippers sought out the great skulls and buried them in stone caskets.

The cave bear was one of the oldest of Animal Masters, but he was by no means the last. In ancient Britain, Celtic tribes paid honor to Cernunnos, lord of the forest, sometimes manifest as a great stag, sometimes as an antlered man, and sometimes in more grotesque guises. As the centuries passed and Britain succumbed again and again to foreign conquerors, this old Animal Master faded from view, until only antique carvings, little understood, showed that he had ever existed. But Cernunnos apparently lived on, ruling in deep forests far from the farms and towns of mortals.

In fact, long after his name had been forgotten by most folk, Cernunnos was seen by a Welsh warrior in the course of his travels. The man, who was called Cynon, son of Clydno, told a group of his fellows that his one glimpse of the Animal Master was the most wondrous thing he had ever known.

The tale Cynon related was this: He had ridden out, as was the custom then, to seek adventure. He traveled far beyond the boundaries of his world, through mountains and along strange shores, and he sheltered at many lords' fortresses. At one, his host told him that if he followed a track to a certain forest and took a particular pathway within it, he would find a marvel.

Being high-spirited and full of curiosity, Cynon investigated. The morning after his conversation, he rode out on a dirt track that led across the barley fields, down a valley and into a wood.

The track through the wood was broad and sunny, but the byway Cynon found was narrow. As he followed it, the air darkened. Ancient trees formed a vault of shadows over his head and a network of grasping roots under his horse's hoofs. He reined in from time to time to listen, but the silence was profound. He heard nothing, not even the usual rustlings that enlivened a forest. Leaves drifted down, but even they were as silent as snowfall. It was as if the forest listened and watched.

The track stopped abruptly, and the air lightened. Cynon had come to a clearing, a small meadow, bright with daisies and loud with bird song. In the center of this clearing was a grassy mound. A large twelve-point stag grazed beside it. The beast raised its head and looked at Cynon, motionless as only a watching animal can be. And in that instant, a creature appeared on the mound.

It was a gigantic man, as dark as a moonless night. The man's two legs were fused into one mass, resting on a single foot. He leaned upon an iron club and regarded Cynon with a single, unblinking eye, sunk deep in his forehead. Despite powerful musculature, he seemed old, perhaps as old as the trees around his clearing, as old perhaps as the sky. He said nothing at all, but his eye was knowing.

"I am Cynon, son of Clydno," announced the young man. To his chagrin, his voice cracked slightly, sliding up above its normal husky pitch. He stood his ground, however.

The dark figure replied only, "Leave this place, mortal."

Cynon persisted. "What powers have you, my lord?"

The response was a movement of the lips that might have been a smile. "Little man, little man," the thing on the mound said slowly, "I will show you what power is." And with his iron club he struck the stag across its neck. The stag threw back its head and bellowed (continued on page 23),

EGYPT'S DIVINE MENAGERIE

In the centuries of Egypt's pharaohs, when great temples rose along the curves of the Nile, the presence of gods was sensed everywhere, even among the animals that crowded the land. The hippopotamus, wallowing amid the river's mud and weeds, housed the spirit of Taweret, who aided childbirth. The crocodile, floating motionless in the Nile shallows, was the incarnation of Sebek, guardian of river life. The sleek cat that basked on sun-warmed temple stones was Bast, goddess of pleasure. Even the frog among the water reeds was thought to be divine. All beasts that walked or swam or flew, it seemed, were charged with more than mortal power. It was therefore not surprising that the highest gods should manifest themselves in varied forms of the mortal beings they ruled. Osiris, supreme lord of creation and order, took the form of a man. His brother Set was evil, a god of chaos; upon the body of a man, Set bore the head of a hyena, creature of the desert and death. Osiris' Queen, Isis, who reigned over the winds, was a woman winged like a falcon; each year those broad and shining wings carried the vivifying breath of spring across the land.

Isis was the lifegiver. Egyptians sang that Set, mighty in his evil strength, slew Osiris and dismembered him and scattered the sacred body throughout the length of Egypt to hide it. It was Isis, ceaselessly mourning, tirelessly searching, who restored her husband to his rightful form and, with her great wings, fanned the breath of life into him that he might speak to her once more. But even Isis could not avert the force of chaos. Osiris retired, as he must, to the underworld, leaving Isis with a son, Horus, the falcon-headed god, to battle Set and his rude power. And while the falcon and hyena fought for heaven's crown, chaos was loosed upon the world.

In the desert, storms raged; on once-rich plains, animals fought their own kind; in the rivers, fish devoured one another. And still the gods fought—for many lifetimes, the story-

tellers said—and the world lay in darkness and disorder.
At last, however, the gods of the world gathered in
judgment—Sebek, the crocodile-headed, and the lesser
gods of field, hearth and village, all led by the lord of balance and justice. The lord was
Thoth, who took the form of the white ibis. And the judgment they gave was this: that Horus
the falcon should rule the world in place of Osiris, his father, and screaming Set should
harness his powers to guard the chariot of the sun, to be forever a servant instead of a lord.

And as for Osiris, he remained eternally separate from Isis, his sorrowing winged
Queen. While Isis flew above the earth and called forth light and life each year at spring-
time, Osiris remained forever in the underworld. His companion there was Anubis, jackal-

headed god of the dead, who judged the human souls that descended to the dark realm. Anubis never saw the sunlight, but the soul of Osiris wandered each day in the upper world. The proof was the ba-bird, seen sometimes in flight above the Nile, sometimes perched on temple walls or palace steps, quietly observing the busy workings of humanity. Its feathers were azure, rimmed with crimson, and its head was that of Osiris, the ruler of the land of death.

loud as the blast of a winter wind. The stag's voice reverberated among the branches of the trees, growing in volume until the land itself seemed to quiver. The birds ceased their singing.

It was a summons, and it was answered. From all around the clearing came sounds – hummings and rustlings and cracklings and whispers. And then, through the tangle of brush and hedge and vine swept a wave – more, a flood – of animals. They came by the thousands. Grass trembled with the slithering of the serpents and bent under the feet of waddling hedgehogs, lithe stoats, prancing hares, foxes, badgers clothed in snowy stripes, dappled fawns. Behind them, great-tusked boars grunted and snuffled, and in the boars' wake came wolves and wildcats.

Cynon's horse blew and whinnied and backed, so that the young man had to keep a rigid hold on the reins. But the creatures ignored both horse and rider. They crowded around the mound where the stag stood and the one-eyed figure leaned on his club.

Then the giant raised his club and spoke in a voice of thunder. "Bow, creatures," he said. And with hardly a sound, each animal touched its head to the ground. Even the snakes rolled on their backs so that they, too, might give obeisance.

Cynon trembled and, unable to resist, bowed his head as well, his mind washed clean of all except the knowledge that he must submit. Then the ancient voice rumbled coldly, "Little mortal, you have seen the power of the lord of the forest. Now leave this place." And the young man did as he was bidden.

So, through some rent in the veil of time, an ancient god showed himself to a mortal of the latter age, a reminder to arrogant humankind that powers from the elder days yet dwelled within the world, even if those powers were not exercised as they once had been. In some times and places, however, when people were closer to the earth, the old magics still thrived and gave to mortal life the richness and the danger of the first world.

One of those places was the Greece of Theseus and the Minotaur, where gods walked among mortals in a range of guises – as bulls, eagles, snakes, goats, stags, rams and foxes, to name only a few. On such easy intimacy were gods, men and animals that the Greeks were fond of describing the neighboring Egyptian deities, half-animal beings, as members of the Greek pantheon who long before had fled to Egypt in animal disguise when pursued by a murderous primal dragon.

In Greece, mortals claimed descent from sacred animals. The Erechtheids – Theseus' clan – were said to have descended from a serpent, and their fortresses always sheltered house snakes that were devotedly fed on honey cakes and milk. Among other powerful mainland clans were the Pallantids, whose ancestral animal seems to have been the goat, and the Leontids, who traced their origin to a lion. Given such lineages, people could readily believe that a Cretan Queen, whose family was strengthened by kinship to bulls, should give birth to a child with the head of a bull.

Of the horse-men known as Centaurs, one was famed for his mastery of the arts
that served humankind. His name was Chiron, and he taught his god-given skills
in music, warfare and the hunt to the bravest heroes—Achilles, Jason and Hercules.

The Greeks viewed with equanimity the shifting and mixing of human and beast shapes. Transformation seemed woven into the very fabric of their lives, so that even common beasts were wreathed in mystery. The nightingale and the swallow, for instance, once had been women. The swallow was Procne, daughter of the King of Athens, and the nightingale was Philomela, her sister.

Their story was a tangled and sorry one. Procne had married Tereus, King of Daulis to the northwest, and borne him a son. Then he discarded her—hiding her and cutting out her tongue so that she could not tell her woe—in favor of Philomela,

who, all unknowing, married him. When the sisters discovered how they had been betrayed, they murdered Tereus' son and served his flesh to the King in a stew. Tereus realized what he had eaten and sought the two women, intending to hack them to death. The gods, however, thinking that the bloodshed had gone on long enough, put an end to it by metamorphosis. Philomela was changed by the gods into nightingale form; in her nocturnal song, she endlessly mourned the murdered child. Procne was transformed into the tongueless swallow; she could only scream and fly in circles, forever trying to evade the crested hoopoe—for that was the bird Tereus became—as it pursued her.

Similar tales were attached to other animals, but not all such histories included kindly intervention on the part of the gods. The fate of Midas, for instance, seems to have been caused by capricious irritation among the divinities.

Midas ruled a small kingdom on the eastern coast of Macedonia. He was a member of a rich, pleasure-loving dynasty and inherited a taste for opulence: Even as a young man, for instance, he had a rose garden that was famed for its splendors. In later life, he was adopted by the childless King of Phrygia, in what is now Turkey, and eventually succeeded to the Phrygian throne. He seems to have been a powerful ruler, but at some point he had the misfortune, it was said, to offend a god. The error was small—he preferred the music of the goat-god Pan to that of the sun-god Apollo—

but the result was indubitably appalling.

The King awoke one morning to the sound of a curious rustling on the linen beneath his head. He turned, and from the corner of his eye saw a streak of brownish gray. It was an ass's ear, long and pointed, laced with little veins, coated and rimmed with gleaming hair. The King ran his hand along it, found its root in his own scalp, and knew the truth: The offended god had adorned him with the animal's ears.

One person, and one person only, saw the King in his affliction: his barber. The man entered the white-walled royal chambers that morning and found his master seated by a window, his face ashen. From the mass of the King's hair, on either side of his head, rose the ass's ears. At every small sound, they flicked inquiringly and involuntarily. The barber's lips twitched at this sight, but he did not laugh. He simply waited for the King to speak.

"Examine them," ordered Midas. His voice had taken on a hoarse, mournful quality, regrettably reminiscent of an ass's sobbing bray.

The barber did as he was told, running his hands over the ears and down to their bases in the King's hair. He found a seamless whole; the flesh of the King's skull was knitted to that of the animal's ears, which harbored a healthy colony of fleas.

The tale has a comical tone because of the nature of the deformity, but it was a deadly serious matter. Mystic power was invested in the person of a king in that age, and in some countries, blemished kings were forced to abdicate. All too aware of the effect that the affliction might have on his own position at court, the barber gave

Lords of their mountain solitudes, the Centaurs lived wild and battle-crowded lives. Unlike
Chiron, greatest of their kind, they fought one another savagely, with hand and hoof.

Midas a means of concealment—a many-folded cap, such as those most Phrygians wore. And, at Midas' command, he swore on his life never to reveal the King's secret.

But the barber was a garrulous man, used to the convivial gossip of the servants' quarters. And this was gossip more delectable than any the barber had known before. He swelled with his secret, he ached with it, and only fear for his life kept him from revealing it.

The King kept to his chambers for some days; the barber saw him every day and suffered in his own silence. After a time, however, he found a solution he thought would bring him peace. He went alone to the banks of a river and dug a hole in the mud of the bank. Then he put his mouth to the earth and, in an agony of relief, whispered the secret: "The King, my master, has the ears of an ass." It was as simple as that. The barber filled the hole

A hero's bloody undoing

Some Centaurs, it was said, derived their power from divine blood that flowed in their veins. So the hero Hercules found—and found too late.

It happened that Hercules married a woman called Deianira, daughter of the King of Calydon. As he traveled with her to his own home, he came to a river that was in flood. Nessus, a Centaur, guarded it. Seeing the young bride beside her husband, he offered to carry Deianira across the water. Hercules surrendered his wife—and Nessus fled, intending to take the woman for his own pleasure. He had barely reached the far bank when Hercules shot an arrow into him. But as Nessus lay dying he made the woman into an instrument of revenge.

"Dip your robe in my blood," he said. "If your husband's love should flag, put the linen near his skin. It is magic blood: It will fire his passion for you." Deianira, young and uncertain and eager for the hero's love, soaked up some of the blood with her robe. Then she rejoined Hercules, and they journeyed on to his home.

Years passed happily, but the time came when Hercules' eye began to rove. Deianira saw this and, in a fit of jealousy, resorted to Nessus' charm. She made a tunic from the blood-stained robe and sent this to her husband. Hercules put it on his body.

Centaur blood was poison to humans; the tunic burned on Hercules' skin and ate the flesh and bone away. In an agony of pain, he commanded a funeral pyre. Then he threw himself upon it and was consumed in flames.

As for Deianira, she hanged herself when she found what she had done. So did creatures of old races visit vengeance on the new.

carefully and went about his business.

Unfortunately for him, the god of that river had ears to hear—and many mouths to speak. The barber's words were caught among the river reeds and sighed out gently whenever the slightest breeze blew, thereby revealing the King's punishment to all who passed.

The barber's own punishment was swift: He was executed. Then Midas, his kingship smirched and his person a laughingstock, killed himself by drinking the blood of sacred bulls. He died in agony: Only the priestesses of the Great Goddess could taste such blood with impunity.

Metamorphosis, no matter how it was caused, was an infrequent recourse of the earliest creative powers. Most of the creatures who roamed the earth were not transformed mortals or oddities patched together from the parts of different species. They were creations in their own right and came from races at least as old as humankind. As much as men and women, they were children of the gods, and some of them were formidable indeed.

Among the most powerful were the Centaurs, a tribe that haunted the forested slopes of Mount Pelion, near the coast of Thessaly in the northern part of Greece. Shepherds and other wanderers occasionally glimpsed one moving along a mountain ridge. They described the Centaur as having a man's head, powerful arms and an arching back; when seen standing motionless among the trees, a Centaur appeared, in fact, to be a man, if a very tall one. But any movement showed the differ-

ence. At the base of the man's spine, the gleaming flesh changed to slick hair, and the spine itself melted into the withers and shoulders of a horse.

The Centaurs were descendants of a mortal who had tried to defile a goddess. The story, in brief, was this: A King of Thessaly named Ixion attempted to seduce the goddess Hera; her consort, Zeus, shaped a false image of her from a cloud; Ixion lay with this phantasm, and from the union was born Centaurus, who—exiled to Mount Pelion—interbred with the wild mares there to produce the Centaur tribe.

Whatever its lineage, the tribe was fierce. Although equine, Centaurs ate raw flesh. And they were driven mad by wine; it turned them into monsters, armed with slashing hoofs and clawing hands.

But one among the Centaurs was more than either man or beast, and his parentage was different from the others. He was Chiron, son of a god and a sea spirit. Men called him the Divine Beast, because he possessed unmatched skills in musicmaking, healing and the arts of war. He served as a tutor to gods and humans both. Among his mortal pupils were Jason, Achilles and Hercules, who would eventually earn great renown as warriors.

The human boys spent long hours astride the Centaur's broad back, riding the cool slopes of the mountains and the plain beyond, and listening gravely to Chiron's songs of earth magic and elemental powers. At night, during the years of their apprenticeships, they sheltered with the Divine Beast in a cave. They never forgot his wisdom or his patient kindness, and even after they had left him to prove themselves among their fellows, they returned to confer and bask once more in the sunny peace that surrounded the Centaur. One of these visits brought the beast his death. Here is how it happened:

Hercules, fresh from triumphs on the battlefield, returned to his old mentor on a summer day, full of tales of glory. Leaning easily on his spear and squinting a little in the dappled shade, Hercules talked and talked. Chiron listened placidly, only raising an eyebrow now and then at the braggadocio. After a while, however, the Centaur walked to the pack horse that carried the weapons of Hercules and, with characteristic curiosity, began to inspect the mortal's gear. From a leather quiver he drew an arrow, turning it over in his hands.

"Have a care, master," said Hercules. "Those arrows are envenomed by magic."

Chiron's heavy brows drew together, but he said merely, "An unnatural trick for a warrior." He dropped the arrow to the ground. It rebounded, and the sharp head grazed his foreleg at the pastern. Scarlet drops appeared on the limb.

Hercules started forward, but even as he moved, the Centaur stumbled and collapsed on the ground, his long legs jerking convulsively and foam bubbling at his mouth. He lay thus for hours, while Hercules watched helplessly and wept, for the poison had no antidote, and Chiron, being immortal, would not die from it. He could only suffer eternal pain.

At length, the Centaur begged the gods for death, and this was mercifully granted. Then, as Hercules watched, Chiron disappeared. The Greeks said that Zeus translated his great frame into stars, to fly forever as the constellation Sagittarius, the wise archer with the Centaur's body.

Thus, even an immortal could succumb to mortals, leaving behind a silent, hollow place, no longer lively with the voices of the first world. But humankind did not seem to realize what the earth was losing. Humans, by their nature, desired to control the world, to find pattern and shape and explanation. This being so, the god-beasts, with their deep magic, could never be fully understood by the mortal mind

Though slain by a mortal warrior's weapon, the Centaur Chiron gained
new life. Through the vault of the heavens he flies as the archer-constellation
Sagittarius, his bow forever drawn against the sparkling, venom-bearing Scorpio.

—could not even be safely contemplated.

The powers of Dionysus—he who sheltered the Cretan Princess Ariadne on the island of Naxos—provide a case in point. This god was the lord of the creative tides that ebb and flow in nature, the master of wild and fecund powers. He roamed restlessly throughout the world, and wherever he went, fountains of milk or wine might spring from the ground. The vine and its releasing pleasures were Dionysus' special gift to the world.

He led a huge band of beings. Some of them were beast-men—eternally lustful and fertile satyrs, whose heads were those of humans and whose legs were those of goats. Some were mortal women, called maenads, or bacchantes. Wearing the masks of lynxes and foxes and lions in his honor (Dionysus took the form of many animals), these women celebrated him in wild mountain dances.

Even though Dionysus was the lord of fierce joys, he was the bloodiest of gods. On some mornings after his rituals, observers would see the celebrants trailing down mountain paths in a state of exhaustion. They dragged their animal masks by the binding strings, their festive robes were in rags, and the pallor of their dull, shocked faces was made more marked by the darkening blood that crusted their mouths and smeared their flesh. Some of them carried tokens of the night's carnage—the limbs or heads of fellow humans, whom the maenads had torn apart in the frenzy of the god. For when mortals denied or resisted Dionysus, the punishment was terrible: The inchoate energies he released created not joyous freedom but untamed, bestial destructiveness and manic illusion, so that in the trances of the dance, mortals saw even their own children as wild animals and ripped them limb from limb.

The elder magic that flowed through Dionysus—magnificent in its vigor, perilous in its unbridled power—was everywhere manifest in the beast-children of the gods, no matter how humble those children might be. Even rustic spirits had something in them too terrifying for mortal eyes to look upon—or so it was said in the Grecian hills where Pan dwelled.

A cheerful shepherd who haunted the rugged mountains of Arcadia in the Peloponnesus, Pan was a goat-god akin to the satyrs of Dionysus, although he preferred a solitary existence to their frenzied carousings. Pan had the head and torso of a man, but his hairy ears were sharply pointed, small horns curled from his forehead, and his shaggy legs ended in glittering cloven hoofs. There was some dispute about his parentage, but all agreed that when the mother saw her hideous infant, with its oddly shaped eyes and goatish limbs, she abandoned it forthwith, expecting that it would perish. The desertion was without effect, however. For centuries, the goat-god roamed the heights with capering ease, a creature perfectly fitted to his lofty world.

He was certainly not without the lustful propensities of his kind. He was said to have lain with every one of Dionysus' maenads during their wild celebrations, and he fathered children on several of the retiring nymphs who guarded trees and mountain pools. But he accepted his failures in this sphere with charming insouciance. It was said that the nymph Pitys escaped him only by changing herself into a fir tree; Pan cut one fragrant bough and wove it into a chaplet to wear in her honor.

And the pipes that echoed across Pan's countryside were a similar souvenir. Attracted by her shyness, Pan pursued Syrinx, a mountain nymph, to the banks of a stream. She flitted in and out of his sight as she ran down the wooded slopes toward the water, for all nymphs were fleet of foot. But he overtook her at last, only to see her dwindle and then vanish among the swaying green reeds. Syrinx had magically become one of them. He searched for a while, but one reed looks much like another, and at last he gave up. He cut several of the hollow stems, however, and bound them together to make his pipes, which sounded a song as sweet as a woman's.

Such were the winter tales that Arcadian shepherds told when they huddled in their domed twig huts during the dark season, hearing the mountain wolves howl high above and the rain blow in the wind. They spoke with affection, for Pan was the guardian of their flocks. He warded off the wolves, and he also drove small game into their bowshot.

The goat-god was never far away. In January, at lambing time, his pipes would sound in the shadows near the sheepfold. Late in March, when the first cuckoo called and the shepherds "armed" – or belled – their animals before driving them into the high pastures for the summer,

Mysterious were the powers of the gods of the first world – too great, it seemed, for mortals to resist. Thus Dionysus, god of growth and of the vine, master of metamorphosis, prince of chaos, gave wild joys to the satyrs and the humans who followed him – and savage punishment to those who denied his divinity.

One who scorned Dionysus was Pentheus, King of Thebes, a strong and rigid man who was angered by the madness of the women of his kingdom when Dionysus walked among them. Naked, they danced among the pines of Mount Cithaeron near the city; Pentheus sought to stop them.

He paid no heed to his advisers, who warned him that mortal order did not rule the world. In his arrogance, Pentheus followed the women one night to the mountain and watched them while they whirled and frolicked. They wore the masks of goats and foxes; fawn skins draped their white shoulders; and more than mortal pleasure glittered in their eyes, for they were free, in that holy trance, from the coils of mortality. Dionysus let the King watch for some moments; then the god unleashed his ancient powers to the full. They were too much for frail mortals to contain: The dancers soared into savagery. They tore goats and cattle into pieces; the sound of their screaming echoed among the trees. Then they found Pentheus where he hid in a pine tree. In their god-inspired madness, they thought him a beast; they fell upon him and rent him limb from limb. His own mother tore off the King's head and, in the morning, carried the bloody relic to Pentheus' palace, believing she cradled the head of a lion.

The madness slowly left the women; they wailed to see what they had done. Dionysus disappeared from Thebes. Thus, said the Greeks, the harsh lesson was given: The time had not yet come when mortals could challenge the powers of the old gods.

he was there just out of eyesight, watching them make ready to come to him.

Summer was his true season. When the sun beat down on the steep Arcadian slopes and blue anemones starred the grass, when the bright light glittered on the wings of circling kestrels, Pan became the watchman. Long, idle hours he lay in the heavy shade of the cypress trees, while far below him, his charges lived their little lives. The shepherds squatted lazily on the grass, their crooks across their knees and their dark eyes watching the slowly eddying flocks of sheep and dancing goats. The sound of their work echoed up the mountainsides into the blue bowl of the sky: Loud in the summer silence came a rhythmless, faraway clanking of bronze sheep bells, occasional sharp whistles from the shepherds, and quick barks from their dogs.

That time of lengthy summer afternoons was safe for mortals while the oblong, leaf brown eyes of the goat-god watched them. They knew he was there. They heard the pipes from time to time, or rustlings among the trees, or the click of hoofs on rock. But they did not see him and did not care to: None but the reckless dared seek out the god.

Some shepherds, however, came upon him by accident. A man might wander from his flock at the hour when the blazing sun stood straight overhead. If he ventured to a glade or clearing where bees hummed in the flowering thyme, he might catch a glimpse of pointed ears. And that glimpse might be his undoing. A shout would pierce the air and beat upon his skull; the hair on his head would rise, and blindness would descend upon his eyes. And if he was found alive after that, he would be witless and whimpering, blasted by the primal power of Pan.

Such things happened only in the childhood of humankind, which, like any childhood, was both safe and full of danger. And like all childhoods, it slowly slipped away. As encroaching humankind grew older and stronger, the beast-children of the gods began to vanish. Some chroniclers believe that the end came during the reign of the Roman Emperor Tiberius, in the first century of the present era, and that it was announced to an Egyptian ship's pilot named Thamus.

His ship, bound for Rome, skirted the western shore of the Peloponnesus. Just off the island of Paxos, the wind dropped and flat calm spread across the sea. Before the galley slaves could unlock their oars, a voice from the island—a divine voice, Thamus later insisted—sent a clarion call across the water.

"Thamus!" it cried.

He peered at the forested shore and heard his own name called twice more. Then Thamus stood in the bow and shouted, "I hear!"

"Tell them that the great god Pan is dead," intoned the voice, and it fell silent.

Unnerved, Thamus' crew set to the oars. At the next landfall—probably Corcyra—Thamus solemnly did as he had been ordered. The gods of Greece were not his gods, but a sensible man took care not to offend unseen powers. He signaled for the oarsmen to lie to. When the ship

lay dead in the water, he cupped his hands to his mouth and shouted the doleful message toward the island.

Then the Egyptians skimmed away from the rugged cliffs. But at their backs they heard a great wail of lamentation, as if each stone and tree and stream of Greece were keening for the goat-god.

Some later said that Thamus had misunderstood the voices; some said that the Christians had invented the tale as proof that their own god now mastered the earth. But Thamus knew what he had heard.

And indeed, the old gods and divine beasts were leaving the civilized world. In the mountains of Arcadia, the laughing pipes of Pan were silenced, although shepherds still insisted that when the wind was right, a ghostly melody fluted among the pines. No longer did the goat-men of the

Amorous as any satyr, the goat-god Pan pursued a nymph but was foiled when she hid among
river reeds and took reed form herself. Conceding defeat, he cut the reeds to make pipes.
When he blew kisses across the hollow stems, the sweetest of melodies sounded.

Across the hills of ancient Ireland slithered, crawled and crept Fomorians, creatures
made of a motley of beast and human flesh. Skilled in enchantment, they
ruled the seas and kept the island under stern and cruel rule.

Aegean world caper in the festivities of Dionysus, although their mystic rites inspired a form of mortal entertainment. In amphitheaters at Athens and elsewhere, men in animal masks appeared in plays, singing *tragedoi* – literally, "goat songs."

On wilder shores, however, beast-creatures long maintained the memory of the old world. But even these straggling survivors of the elder days eventually found themselves in opposition to a newer, stronger race.

Such was the case in Ireland. That island, remote in its gray sea, was richly green and rolling. Fat trout leaped in its streams, and stags called on its mountains; the valleys were crowded with hazel woods and thickly berried bushes. It was welcoming country for strangers, and as its legends tell, it was settled repeatedly by competing tribes. At the time of its most famous early conflict, there were three.

The challenging race was the Tuatha Dé Danann, thought to be magicians or perhaps even gods. They certainly were of more than mortal beauty, although of human form. They had come from northern lands that no one had seen, arriving in a mist that blanketed Ireland for days.

The Tuatha had found two peoples inhabiting the island. By a series of battles and treaties too complicated to describe, they had come to share the land with them in uneasy peace. One group, a tribe said to have descended from fugitive Greek slaves, was unable to withstand the others; they were sent to occupy a patch of ground in the west of the country. The other group was powerful, and to these beings the Tuatha paid tribute. The

Tuatha lords even intermarried with them, although they were a curious race indeed.

They were called Fomorians, and it was thought that they once had been sea rovers in the oceans off Africa. Whatever their origins, they were a tatterdemalion remnant of the chaotic powers of creation. Some had a single leg and a single eye. Some had men's bodies and the sleek heads of horses. Some looked like fish, scaled and oblong, but walked upright on flipper-like feet, their doleful human faces peering from bullet heads. A very few were beautifully human, at least in form.

The warlike Fomorians dominated Ireland, living by taxes imposed on the bounty of the country's fields and pastures, although they preferred to remain secluded in their stronghold, an island off the northwest coast. The place was an awesome sight from the sea. At its center rose a tower as translucent as glass, and within this tower, according to the chroniclers, could be seen "something that had the appearance of men." Those who ventured too near the island-fortress might find their ships swamped by spell-sent waves.

The chief of the Fomorian tribe was named Balor of the Strong Blows. He was a cyclops, and the single eye he had was kept shut. Its very glance killed. In time of ultimate need during a battle, his guides would lift his eyelid with an ivory ring, and all who met that gaze died where they stood, inwardly seared by some nameless power from the dawn of creation.

Balor had a grandson who was to prove

his bane. The boy was the child of a secret union between Balor's daughter—who possessed the human beauty seen in some Fomorians—and a warrior of the Tuatha. When Balor discovered the child, he had him cast into the sea in his swaddling clothes, for it was prophesied that Balor would meet his end at the hands of his own grandson. But the child was rescued by chiefs of the Tuatha—his kin—and reared in secret for fear of Fomorian wrath.

When this child grew to be a man, he presented himself to the Tuatha King in Ireland. In the young man, the powers of the older races evidently had been channeled into human skills, and these skills were formidable: He was a warrior, a poet, a harper, a sorcerer, a physician, a brassworker and smith. There was, in fact, no creative skill known then that he did not possess. Moreover, it was said that his face was like a god's—so wise and shining that (as with his grandfather's evil eye) no mortal could bear to look upon it. The young man was called Lugh of the Long Hand because of his strength, and he was made the champion of the Tuatha, that he might free them from Fomorian rule.

His first action in the pursuit of freedom was murder. The day came when the tribute gatherers of the Fomorians approached the Tuatha King's fortress to demand their due. They were a frightening lot of creatures, some hairless and simian, some goatish, some round and red as if the clay they were made of was not fully dried. One, its visage covered by a cloth of white and its body by long draperies, sat astride a horse, but its feet dangled below the animal's belly, and those feet were clawed.

And there in the courtyard of the fortress, Lugh of the Long Hand hacked them all to death, save nine. Those nine he sent to Balor, to tell what had happened and who had done the deed. Then he began the work of mustering the armies of the Tuatha for the battle that must come.

It came soon enough. When Balor heard the tale of the tribute gatherers, he called together his sea rovers and his warriors. In ships with painted sails, the company descended on Ireland and tore across the country, killing as they went.

They met the host of the Tuatha on the plain at Mag Tured, in the Connacht region of Ireland. The fighting continued for days, but Lugh of the Long Hand was not in it at first: The Tuatha King, fearing for the champion's life, sequestered him under guard. Because of this, the battle went badly for the Tuatha—until the champion broke away from the men around him and rallied the field.

Then the slaughter was terrible. "Many comely men fell there in the stall of death," wrote the chronicler. "Pride and shame were there side by side and hardness and red anger, and there was red blood on the white skin of young fighting men. And the dashing of spear against shield, and sword against sword, and the shouting of the fighters and the whistling of spears and the rattling of scabbards, was like thunder through the battle. And many slipped in the blood that was under their feet, and they fell, striking their heads against one another; and the river carried away bodies of friends and enemies together."

The reign of Ireland's Fomorians—relics of an early age—was ended one dark day on the plain of Mag Tured. The conquerors were the warriors of a brave new race, the Tuatha Dé Danann, led by the Prince known as Lugh of the Long Hand.

The dog-men of the Andaman Isles

Even as magical beasts grew rare in the Western world, they flourished in remote corners of the earth — or so travelers' tales would suggest. The Italian wanderer Marco Polo, for instance, reported that a society of canine people inhabited the Andaman Islands, in the Andaman Sea off the coast of Burma. These creatures engaged in a prosperous trade with India. Although it was said that they sometimes devoured mortals, their usual diet was peaceful fare: rice, nuts, apples and milk.

Then Lugh of the Long Hand found his grandfather, Balor. The Fomorian chief stood in a battle chariot, surrounded by gibbering, squealing, howling warriors of his army. His enormous eye was still closed; until now, the Fomorians had not thought they would need this greatest of their weapons. The young man shouted a challenge, and Balor leaped to the ground. The warriors around the pair backed away.

Balor said, "Lift my eyelid, that I may see the chatterer." His guides advanced and extended the ivory ring they used to do this. At that instant, Lugh cast his spear. It flew straight to the mark with such force that it skimmed through Balor's skull and into the Fomorians behind, carrying with it fragments of the deadly eye and an arching spout of blood. And every creature the exploding eye touched or the blood spattered died screaming.

Then the rout began. Leaderless, the Fomorians fled, and the men of the Tuatha followed. In the end, only four members of that great army survived. It was said that these four were at last driven from Ireland by a prince of the Tuatha and disappeared to islands in the northern sea.

The Fomorians, perhaps the last of the powerful old order to be vanquished by the new, seem to have been destined for death in any case. They were a weakened race, their people a haphazard collection of beast parts randomly and hideously united, their powers diminished and their dominance maintained not by magic, in the main, but by simple force of arms. The four surviving Fomorians, hidden away on their cold islands, were never seen again. Had any human come across them, the hapless creatures would doubtless have been regarded as nothing more than loathsome curiosities.

That was the invariable fate of the god-beasts who roamed the earth when it was young. They disappeared. Not in glory. Not in some divine display of valor or unconquerable greatness. They retreated from human view, or were sent into exile, or were killed, or simply died. Humankind was heir to the future.

And what was left? Nothing more, it seemed, than a collection of rumors and travelers' tales of far-off lands — garbled visions of piteous creatures that probably existed only in the imaginations of the writers. For the travelers and writers — Greeks such as Herodotus and Ctesias of Cnidus, and their later imitators — did not see the grandeurs that still existed in the hidden corners of the world. They related incredible descriptions of grotesqueries in almost-human form.

Instead of the grace and power of the Centaurs or the might of the stag-god Cernunnos, they reported — on the basis of the most suspect evidence — savage tribes of dog-headed men, ugly and inarticulate, who barked rather than talking. Instead of the wild gaiety of capering Pan, they offered tales of dull monsters: people whose ears grew to the ground and could be used as blankets; sciapods, each with one enormous foot, which could be used as a sunshade; men whose faces grew upon their chests and people who appeared normal except that they had long tails.

Theirs was a dreary recital, indeed. In their world, after all, humankind ruled. That beasts could have godlike potency was an unwelcome thought. They did not know that wonders were still present, that in India and China animals still held sway over men, that in the wild reaches of Russia flew birds with more than avian or human power. And while they heard and wrote of the unicorn, which still shyly lurked in their own dense forests, not one man in a million had seen it or knew its true power and beauty.

The tale of the Monkey-God: An ... for Earthly Supremacy

Storytellers in India remember a time, deep in the past, when the safety of all of creation was at risk and a great war was fought to save it. These dire events began with the abduction of a woman named Sita, wife of Prince Rama, who was called The Azure because the blood of the sky deity was said to flow in his veins. Sita disappeared from her husband's forest retreat, leaving nothing behind but a scattering of jewels. With his brother Laksh-mana, Rama combed the depths of the forest, but no sign of the woman did they find, and all they heard and saw were the chattering voices and leaping shadows of the monkeys that played among the leaves. The monkeys, however, saw all and heard all, and at last they led the brothers to a kingdom hidden beneath the forest. There the

simian warrior-god Hanuman told where Sita was.

Formed like a monkey, with the heart and courage of a god, Hanuman had discovered Sita imprisoned in a golden citadel on an island in the southern sea; Sita's captor was a creature of the other world, a lord of chaos and death. Many-headed, many-armed and charged with evil, he was called Ravana, and he led an army of malformed sprites. Inflamed with desire for the mortal Princess's beauty, he had leaped the walls that shielded the good earth from his disordered realm and seized the woman for his own.

In Hanuman's kingdom, men and monkeys took council. They decided to join forces, for all were threatened by Ravana and his kind. Then Hanuman summoned animal allies from every corner of India and, with his great army, marched to India's southern shore. Men and beasts together built a causeway to the enchanted isle and placed Ravana's citadel under siege.

But they had not reckoned on the awful powers of the many-headed King. Safe in his golden tower, he sent battalions of demonic warriors against the invaders. Some were invisible and could move faster than any earthly creature. Under their onslaught Hanuman's forces fell back, suffering heavy losses and filled with dismay.

When Hanuman saw this, he soared high above the clamor of the battle, above the little island, into the cool and quiet of the clouds. Through a sea of white vapor the monkey-god flew, into the Indian mountains. He alighted in a place where healing herbs grew in abundance. It is said that, in

his haste to supply succor to his forces, he did not pick the herbs but instead tore off a whole mountaintop and carried it back toward the battle.

As he flew over the land, such was the rush of wind and vastness of his burden that humans below thought him a storm. But one man tried to shoot him from the sky. Hanuman spoke in the

voice of thunder and told his mission, and so passed safely on.

As he descended toward the enchanted isle, the scent of the herbs he carried drifted down over his compatriots. Instantly they rallied, swarming against Ravana's army.

Then Ravana's ranks began to fail. Observing this from his citadel, the demon sent his brothers into the fray. They fell before the fury of Rama and Hanuman. At last the lord of chaos went forth himself, his many arms flailing, his teeth gleaming in the sun. Smoke rose from his bow, and he

loosed arrow after arrow into the ranks of Hanuman and Rama. Each arrow writhed in the air, and where it fell appeared a hissing serpent, which slid among the forces of the people of the earth and filled them with terror.

An answer came at once, however — and from the mortal, Prince Rama, who was empowered now, it seemed, with magic. Rama flung a spear into the air, and in its falling the spear loosed a flock of vulture-headed fighters, which swooped down upon serpent and demon-warrior alike, breaking the last resistance of King Ravana's evil hordes.

Although his forces were in ruin and his enchantments undone, Ravana did not yet acknowledge defeat. From each of his mouths came a rolling cry, loud as thunder, cold as death. He surged forward in his battle chariot, intending to destroy Rama. But Rama's spear pierced him, and the mortal's sword severed his many necks. One by one, the heads of Ravana sailed above the remains of his army, spewing arcs of blood.

So the mortal and the monkey-god conquered the demon-lord and delivered Sita from captivity. All through their lives, they remained heart's companions. And such was the goodness of Hanuman's spirit that all who heard of what he did for the mortal race in that dark hour were said to be blessed with his virtue.

Chapter Two

B Riders of the Wind

Before true magic left the world, a white reflection would sometimes skim over the waters of Greece's Gulf of Corinth; a shadow would dance across nearby wheat fields more swiftly than any cloud could move. Then the fishermen would look up from their nets and the goatherds from their flocks, squinting into the bright light. They knew what they would see: Pegasus, the winged horse of the heavens, was at play in his cloud meadows. On great wings he rode the wind. His crescent hoofs tore the clouds to tatters and sent their pale streaks drifting across the blue. In his swooping and soaring, in the wingbeats that carried him higher than the fishermen's and goatherds' eyes could follow, he was a master of the air, more free than earth-tethered mortals could ever be. Mount Helicon, rising on the northern shore of the Gulf of Corinth, was his terrestrial home, but he was often glimpsed in the skies above the city-state of Corinth across the gulf, and the people there honored him. They struck his image on their coins.

A beast of the gods, Pegasus was god-like in his power. Only one man ever harnessed him: Bellerophon the Valiant, son of the King of Corinth. This is his tale:

In his youth, Bellerophon killed a kinsman by accident, perhaps in the battle drills that young men practiced then. Accident or no, Bellerophon had blood guilt on his head, and a time of wandering began for him as he sought to cleanse himself of the stain by exile. He left his home and traveled alone down the Peloponnesus to Tiryns as a suppliant to its King, Proteus. Because of Bellerophon's royal blood, because of his grace and bravery, and because it was the custom, King Proteus welcomed him and gave him the freedom of his court.

But the King's wife observed Bellerophon's grace, too. She took to watching him when he paced the palace yards with the warriors of her husband's court; she even spied on the exercise grounds when he was there practicing with sword and spear. Finally, she found him alone one evening and offered herself as his lover.

"I would not think to dishonor your husband, lady," answered Bellerophon. Without further ceremony, he turned on his heel and left her.

If he had been older and wiser, perhaps, Bellerophon would not have scorned the Queen so harshly. Within the hour she was in her husband's chamber, weeping and trembling. She told Proteus that Bellerophon had tried to rape her, and the King believed what she said. She had long been his wife, after all, and Bellerophon was little more than a handsome stranger.

King Proteus now was caught in a dilemma. His instinct was to avenge himself on the young man—but that man was a royal hearth guest. The dishonor of killing him would have been as great as the dishonor done to the Queen: It would pollute Proteus' house.

The King, who was subtle by temperament, therefore bided his time, saying nothing to the Corinthian until some weeks had passed. Then he honored Bellerophon with a royal mission: He asked him to carry a message across the sea to the Queen's father, Iobates, King of Lycia in Asia Minor. The message was inscribed on a clay tablet in characters that Bellerophon did not understand. The cipher read as follows: "Execute the bearer of this tablet. He has violated my wife and your daughter. Proteus."

Iobates received the stranger hospitably. Only after the young man had been bathed and fed at the royal table did the King ask his business.

"I bear greetings from your son-in-law, Proteus of Tiryns," said Bellerophon, handing the clay tablet to the King. Then he courteously withdrew to a window to give his host privacy for reading. He watched hawks spiral high over the fields beyond the window while Iobates spent long moments studying the tablet.

Finally, King Iobates spoke: "Do you know the message you have brought me?"

"No, lord," Bellerophon said. "That is King Proteus' business and yours. I serve only as the herald, by the King's order."

"This message concerns you, however," Iobates replied. "Proteus wishes me to set you a test of valor." The Lycian King had pondered the matter carefully as he read and reread the tablet. His face revealed nothing of the fury he felt toward the young man he now addressed, nor of the exasperation his son-in-law's tactics had stirred in him. Proteus, shirking the conflicting demands of honor, had ordered that he murder a man who was not only a guest but a messenger—and the person of any messenger was inviolate. Iobates had no intention of staining his own honor, whatever Proteus claimed the man had done. It was better to send Bellerophon into danger and let fate mete out the necessary punishment.

Bellerophon knew nothing of this, of course. His eyes brightened at the thought of danger and fame. "I am honored, lord," he said, and listened intently while Iobates told him the trial.

He was to find and destroy a creature that was ravaging the Lycian countryside. No one was sure of its nature: It was called the Chimera, a word that meant "goat," and some said it was indeed a monstrous goat. Some claimed it was a lion, however, and some a serpent. Some said all three.

The beast laired in the mountains at the borders of the kingdom, and the province there had been blasted back to wilderness. Smoke hung over the scorched and blackened earth, and swollen, headless cattle lay rotting in the roads. No one lived in the region: The few refugees who had straggled to the King's fortress told of screaming in the night, of children gutted by enormous claws and houses destroyed in explosions of fire. Iobates had sent warriors to the mountains to slay the monster, but none of them returned.

All of this Iobates told Bellerophon, giving him fair warning of the difficulties of finding the Chimera and of daring its power. "No one can approach this beast," said the King. "The only creatures that still live in the province are birds, which can fly clear of its fire and claws."

"Just so," Bellerophon replied, and asked for a month to complete his task. Bellerophon was a Corinthian, and all his life he had seen Pegasus caracoling in the clouds above his city. With the arrogance of youth, he thought now to break the winged horse to his service and ride it in pursuit of the Chimera.

Accordingly, he sailed for home. Some chroniclers later said he searched Mount Helicon to find the home of Pegasus, but most believed that one morning he traced the beast's dawn flight to the mountain called Acrocorinthus, which rose steeply from the plain surrounding Corinth. When he saw the horse disappear among the crags, Bellerophon climbed the mountain alone, and in a small meadow near the crest, by a spring that bubbled from the rock, he found Pegasus drinking quietly.

The horse raised his head when Bellerophon stepped onto the grass, and man and beast gazed at each other. The horse's wings were furled along his back; only his white mane stirred slightly, moved by the same mountain breeze that lifted Bellerophon's hair. From the young man's hand dangled a bridle, worthy of the cloud creature that stood before him. It was made of beaten gold, so curiously wrought that it seemed to give off its own light. Storytellers later said that a goddess had given this bridle to Bellerophon, which was why the horse did not take flight at once.

The man raised the bridle and shook it gently, as he would have done to summon his own horses from pasture. But Pegasus had never been bridled. The horse stamped once and blew, and that was all.

Bellerophon took a step forward; the horse backed and roused his wings, and the man at once froze in place. Then, with apparent unconcern, Pegasus lowered his head and tore up a mouthful of grass. Bellerophon approached again, and again the horse retreated.

This stately dance went on and on. At last, when the sun stood high in the heavens, Bellerophon gave up, too tired to continue. But when Bellerophon ceased to try to take, the gods' horse gave. Treading daintily as a lady's riding mare, Pegasus approached and bent his silky head to the bit and bridle. His warm breath smelled of wild flowers.

He shied once, when Bellerophon grasped his mane. But the Corinthian had been bred to riding. He gathered the reins and pulled the horse's head around toward his own, so that Pegasus felt the edge of the gold in his mouth. Instantly, the winged horse quieted. And when Bellerophon leaped upon his back and Pegasus felt the man's weight and the pressure of his thighs, he stood like a stone, awaiting the signal to move.

Bellerophon paused for a moment and looked around. What he saw in the clear mountain air was to remain in his mind's eye all his life: the horse's white head and mane and shoulder, the gleaming edge of the folded wing; the meadow around them, and the columbine, blue and white as sea and cloud, that nestled in the rocks at the meadow's verge. Beyond the rocks, two thousand feet below, spread a plain, gold and green with field and orchard. Beyond the plain stretched blue immensities of water and sky.

Bellerophon tightened his knees and shifted his weight forward. Obedient, as if he had been trained to this, the horse walked ahead. Bellerophon sat back; Pegasus halted. Together, man and horse circled the little meadow: at a walk, at a trot, at a canter. Then Bellerophon turned the horse toward the rocky rim.

"Now!" he shouted, hearing fear and joy in his own voice. He urged Pegasus into a gallop. At the instant they reached the edge, Bellerophon threw himself forward, but the command was unneeded: Pegasus would not refuse the air. The iron muscles gathered under the rider; the horse leaped, and his great wings snapped out to seize the wind.

They were in flight. After a few giddy moments, Bellerophon loosened his fingers—which, he discovered, were tightly twined in Pegasus' mane—and gave the horse his head. They banked and circled the mountain crest. Below, near their aeries, hawks wheeled and screamed shrill defiance. The little mountain meadow among the rocks flashed by and receded, and with a sudden burst of energy, Pegasus shot far upward, until they were sailing among snowy mountains of cloud.

But mortals could not survive at that height for long. After a few moments, Bellerophon shivered and gasped in the thin air. The horse, feeling the tremor, angled down through a cloud mass and out into the sunlight again. Both man and beast emerged from the gloom of the cloud's interior covered with droplets of water, but their swift passage through the air quickly dried them.

Then they headed south and east. With powerful strokes, Pegasus rowed the air, carrying them over the Isthmus of Corinth, past the purple cliffs of Cape Sounion, over the sparkling Aegean and its brown mountain-islands, each peak wreathed with a coronet of cloud. Dusk came and then night, and the earth sliding past below them was curtained by darkness, specked occasionally with tiny lights from island villages. At last they reached the Asian shore, marked by golden points that were the Lycian King's coastal watch fires. A little later, Pegasus descended to the fortress of Iobates. There he alighted, so that Bellerophon might rest and arm himself. The horse did not linger, however, having a dislike of the dwellings of mortals. He took to the sky at once and tirelessly circled in the darkness until he was needed again.

In the morning, before the people of the fortress stirred, Pegasus was waiting for

Borne aloft on the back of Pegasus, the winged horse of the gods, Bellerophon of Corinth assailed the triple-headed monster called the Chimera in its smoky mountain lair.

China's bejeweled herald

In the Orient once dwelled the Fêng-huang, a bird believed to be kindred to the sun and sometimes called the Chinese Phoenix. Its feathers were so beautifully varied in hue that they were said to be infused with the lights of paradise. Its call consisted of five notes that formed a perfect melody. As for its graceful manner of flight, one scholar declared that it "enriches the serenity of the heavens."

This wonderful creature appeared to mortals as a herald of ages of prosperity and peace; it was seen in the skies when great Emperors ascended to the Chinese throne. Then its bell-like notes echoed on every mountainside, even after the bird disappeared to the cloud palaces of the gods.

Bellerophon, who slipped past the guardsman at the gates to join him. The Corinthian was hardly mounted before Pegasus surged into a gallop, forelegs reaching far ahead, heavy hoofs drumming the earth as he found the speed that would carry him into the air. The white wings spread once more, and they were soaring inland, toward the smoky, distant pall that marked the Chimera's wasteland.

They flew low at first, but as they neared the region, Pegasus ascended above the stench that hung over the blackened earth, above the bloated, lazily circling vultures, and up into the mountains.

The smell and the charred branches of the trees made it easy to backtrack the Chimera to its lair. Under Bellerophon's guiding hand, Pegasus curved up through mountain passes, along slopes of scree, past jagged peaks. Finally horse and rider came to a gorge dim with smoke and loud with flies. Pegasus checked at the edge, then glided down into the gap. Bellerophon shouted a battle cry.

Something moved among the shadowed rocks below them; fire flashed. Then the beast came into clear view. It was a lion, furred and clawed, but larger than a horse—larger even than Pegasus himself. From one shoulder grew a horned goat's head, long of tooth and glittering of eye, and this head twisted upward, staring at the winged horse and its rider. From the Chimera's haunch a writhing snake protruded; its mouth was open, baring its fangs, and it hissed at the intruders. The thing was a travesty of nature, an evil joke left over from a time of chaos.

Pegasus screamed and kicked himself upward. Bellerophon let the horse recover, beating in circles in the higher air, while he unslung the bow he carried on his back and nocked an arrow into it. Then he gave the command, and Pegasus, valorous as Bellerophon himself, wheeled and plunged into the gorge where the beast waited. He flew in slow circles, cramped by the narrow space. Below, the lion reared and spat gouts of fire upward; the snake head spewed black venom; the goat head howled. Bellerophon let fly an arrow and nocked another. Fire shot upward, searing his bare calf and causing the horse to veer. But neither horse nor rider quailed. Pegasus darted and leaped like a dragonfly; the man sent

A fatal ascent into the empyrean

From earliest times, mortals watching birds swoop and soar dreamed of gaining the power of flight. One who succeeded was the Athenian Daedalus, a master artisan and servant to King Minos of Crete.

Daedalus was a quarrelsome and arrogant man. He was exiled from Athens for murdering an apprentice in jealousy. Making his way to Crete along with his only son, Icarus, he built the Labyrinth for Minos (pages 6-7). But he offended the King, and both he and Icarus were imprisoned.

No prison could hold Daedalus for long, for there was magic in his hands. He made two pairs of wings, their feathers held together by twine and wax. Then he and his son put them on and left the island, flying northeast over the glittering sea.

Daedalus kept close to the waves, but Icarus was enchanted with his new-found power and desired to climb to the highest reaches of the firmament. With mighty wingbeats, he rose, flying ever nearer to the sun, although his father cried a warning.

Daedalus called too late. The sun's heat melted the wax that glued the wings of the youth. The feathers pulled apart, and wind whistled through the loosening pinions as Icarus plummeted to his death. It was said that sea nymphs wept to see the loss of such beauty and bravery.

As for Daedalus, he circled until Icarus' body floated to the surface. Then he retrieved his son and buried him on the island later called Icaria, in honor of the mortal who had tried for more than mortal power.

arrow after arrow into the howling, screaming thing below.

Then there was silence, except for the beating of the horse's wings and the harsh breathing of the rider. Gradually, the stinging smoke thinned and drifted upward. The Chimera lay twitching in a pool of blood. An arrow protruded from one lion eye; the snake and goat heads hung limp. Bellerophon drew his sword, touched the horse's sides with his heels, and they descended to the stony floor of the gorge. With one swinging blow of the sword, the Corinthian cut off the lion head to make a war trophy. This done, he and Pegasus left that place.

Bellerophon presented the lion head to Iobates as proof of his valor, and in the months that followed, with Pegasus as his mount, he fought for the King against the enemies of Lycia. Such was his courage and so magnificent his mastery of the great winged steed that Iobates came to doubt the charge against him. At last, the King told Bellerophon of the message on the tablet; he received for reply the truth of what had happened at Proteus' court. The King begged the Corinthian's forgiveness for wronging him, and he subsequently made Bellerophon his heir.

Bellerophon might then have had a long and happy life, except that, having commanded the gods' winged horse and flown beyond the reach of mortal eyes, he forgot that he was mortal. Seeking to emulate the gods themselves, he forced Pegasus to fly to Olympus, where only gods might tread. The horse obeyed, but reluctantly. When they neared the peak, the very air seemed to tremble with ancient light and power. Then, as if stung — which indeed, some storytellers said he was — Pegasus shied and screamed and threw the mortal from his back. Bellerophon did not die; his fall to the mountain flank was not great. But he was grievously maimed. His eyes were pierced by the thorns that grew on the mountain, and his bones broken by its boulders. He spent the remainder of his life earthbound, a blind and crippled beggar, outcast by humankind for his arrogance in the face of the gods.

Yet Bellerophon had known glory be-yond what even the bravest man ever found. He had left the earth far behind and sported among the clouds; when he guided the flights of Pegasus, he was invincible. It is no wonder that poets sang of his deeds for centuries.

Of all the creatures of the first world, those that mastered the air were the most wonderful in the eyes of humankind. Unrestrained by gravity, free from the dull round of dailiness, able to traverse limitless distances, they commanded mortal awe. And some indeed were awesome — winged monsters such as the griffins that lived in the mountains of the Caucasus, the Simurgs of Persia and the giant Rocs of the Indian Ocean. Some were feathered creatures of surpassing splendor — the Phoenix of Arabia, for example, or the Firebird of Russia. Some wore the guise of humbler birds seen every day — swans, ravens, geese and wrens; but in those days, and even in later years, those seeming birds were charged with more than avian power. It was impossible for mortals to tell whether a bird was merely a bird, or something more; thus all winged beasts acquired an aura of power.

Some of the oldest and rarest of winged creatures were the most fearsome, for they had not only the freedom of flight, but also the uncontrollable savagery that sometimes marked the dawn of the world.

Among them were the Harpies — or "snatchers" — that lived, it was said, in a cave on Crete but haunted Grecian lands as far north as Thrace. These creatures had the heads and breasts of cruelly emaciated women and the wings and clawed talons of vultures. They gave off a loathsome,

deathly stench and were invariably associated with disaster. As implied by their names – Ocypete (rapid), Celeno (blackness) and Aello (storm) – tempests followed them. And they ravaged the land wherever they went, for it was their fate to be always starving.

The Harpies settled once in Salmydessus, in Thrace, destroying the crops and bringing the people to the brink of starvation. The King of that country, Phineus, a blind man, was tormented ceaselessly by them – a punishment, people whispered, for arrogance. Phineus had the gift of prophecy and once had revealed secrets that only gods should know.

Or so it was said. King Phineus' life was hellish, in any case, for whenever food was spread before him, the Harpies appeared in his chambers, cackling and screaming, their clawed talons clutching at the meat and bread. What they did not take, they befouled. Phineus and his people were helpless against them. The country lay, it seemed, under a hideous spell.

It happened that the Thessalian Prince Jason – he who had been sheltered and schooled by the Centaur Chiron (*page 24*) – came to Salmydessus with a company of the finest warriors of Greece. This band was called the Argonauts because the fifty-oared ship they sailed in – the *Argo* – had been built by a man named Argus. Their mission was to acquire the fabled Golden Fleece of the kingdom of Colchis, on the Black Sea, and they had come to Thrace to seek the advice and prophecy of Phineus.

The Greeks found not the prophet-king they sought but a trembling wreck of a man huddled in the ruins of his palace. Phineus could barely speak; his blind face turned continually from side to side, seeking the direction of the shadow creatures that plagued him.

Their next attack came soon enough. Attracted by the disturbance the young men made – and by the smell of their provisions – the Harpies descended through the shattered roof of Phineus' hall. Screaming with rage and covetousness, beating the air with heavy black wings, they headed straight for the King.

But this time they were defeated: Jason's men were strong and determined; they had no fear of winged women. A pair of warriors sprang forward to protect the old King with their shields. Two others faced the Harpies. These two were Calais and Zetes; it was later said that they themselves were winged, although this may have been poets' embroidery. In any event, they beat the creatures back from the King. The Harpies, gibbering and howling, flew out of the hall, and Calais and Zetes gave chase. With sword and spear, they drove the sisters from the land.

It was said that the Harpies retreated to their cave in Crete and menaced humankind no more. But sometimes at night, people in the surrounding countryside would hear their vicious cackling and see their black forms skimming across the starry sky, heading no one knew where.

Phineus was suitably grateful for his deliverance. He told Jason and the Argonauts how to navigate the Black Sea to reach Colchis, and he revealed what he

A feathered protector of princes

Among Persian birds, the monarch was the Simurg, a jewel-like creature whose feathers had powers of healing. Poets said it guarded the families of Persian heroes, and they told this tale:

Once, a son was born to a lordly warrior and given the name Zal. He was a beautiful child, save that his hair was as white as a goose's wing, a deformity so ill-omened that his father took the infant into the mountains, to expose him to the mercies of the beasts of prey. But the child did not die: The Simurg found him and carried him to its aerie to care for him throughout his infancy and boyhood. When the boy was of age, the enchanted bird returned him to his father, and such had been Zal's schooling in the mountains that the youth was at once given the honor he deserved.

The bird then disappeared, but it left behind one of its iridescent feathers, to protect Zal throughout his life. And when Zal married and begot a child, it was the presence of the feather that made the delivery safe and gave the child the strength of heroes. That child was Rustam, greatest of Persian warriors, a slayer of dragons and the protector of his people.

Black-winged Harpies — foul daughters of death and darkness — tormented the
blind King Phineus of eastern Thrace. Only the warriors of the hero
Jason were able to defy them and give the frail King rest at last.

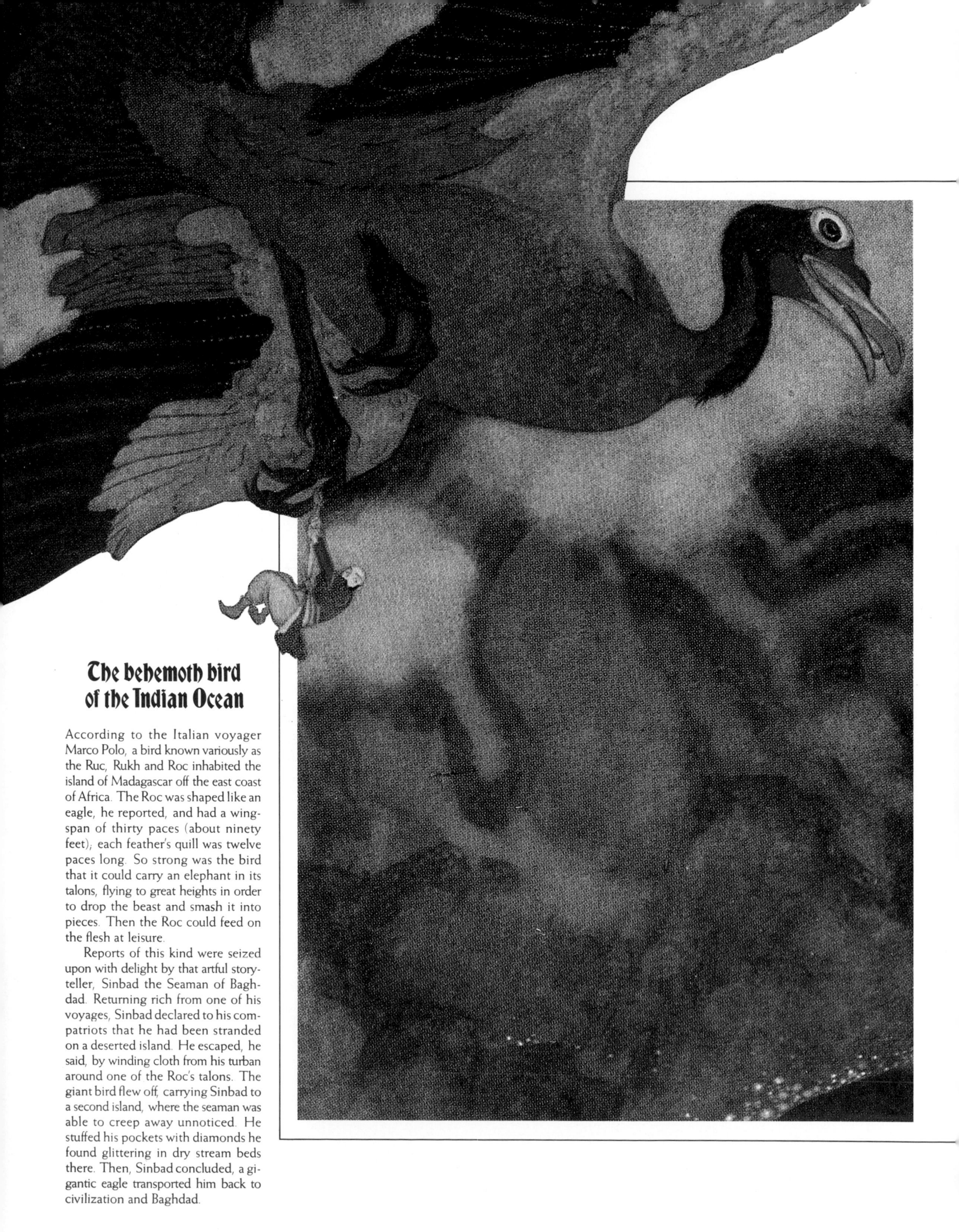

The behemoth bird of the Indian Ocean

According to the Italian voyager Marco Polo, a bird known variously as the Ruc, Rukh and Roc inhabited the island of Madagascar off the east coast of Africa. The Roc was shaped like an eagle, he reported, and had a wing-span of thirty paces (about ninety feet); each feather's quill was twelve paces long. So strong was the bird that it could carry an elephant in its talons, flying to great heights in order to drop the beast and smash it into pieces. Then the Roc could feed on the flesh at leisure.

Reports of this kind were seized upon with delight by that artful story-teller, Sinbad the Seaman of Baghdad. Returning rich from one of his voyages, Sinbad declared to his compatriots that he had been stranded on a deserted island. He escaped, he said, by winding cloth from his turban around one of the Roc's talons. The giant bird flew off, carrying Sinbad to a second island, where the seaman was able to creep away unnoticed. He stuffed his pockets with diamonds he found glittering in dry stream beds there. Then, Sinbad concluded, a gigantic eagle transported him back to civilization and Baghdad.

knew of the dangers that might await them. When the Argonauts had resumed their journey, King Phineus set about putting his kingdom to rights, and in after years, he and his people prospered.

Defeat taught the Harpies to fear humankind, but certain other of the winged beasts of ancient days were naturally shy of mortals. Sensing the threat that humans posed, they lived out their lives in remote wildernesses. Such was the case with griffins. Images of these curious-looking creatures—regal lions with eagles' wings and heads, and long, pointed ears—appeared in strongholds all over Greece and, later, throughout Europe, painted on pottery, carved on palace walls, sculpted into stone guardians of towers.

It was said that griffins pulled the chariots of the gods, that their feathers had the power of curing blindness, that their enormous claws could be made into drinking cups whose surfaces darkened in color in the presence of poison. But few people in the civilized world ever saw the beasts, which reportedly laired in the wilds of Asia. There was even disagreement about their shape. Some accounts held that griffins were black-feathered all over, except for their breasts, which were red. Others claimed that they were white-winged, with blue neck feathers. Still others recorded golden griffins, whose wings glittered with every color of the spectrum.

One man who left a description of griffins—perhaps the first person to do so—was an eccentric Greek who wrote almost three thousand years ago. He was named Aristeas, and his home was Proconnesus, a Greek island colony in the Pro-pontis, the small sea between Thrace and Phrygia—now called the Sea of Marmara.

Aristeas was a wanderer, given to sudden disappearances from his home when restlessness gripped him. He left Proconnesus one day and traveled north, and six years passed before he returned. Then he had wonders to tell. Aristeas had traveled into central Asia through the land of the Scythians—rich nomadic tribesmen who inhabited what is now southern Russia. He had crossed the windy steppes with them, venturing into the bleak mountains of the Caucasus. There he dwelled with the Issedonians, a tribe of long-haired people who were said to devour the flesh of their dead parents and to preserve the skulls. From them Aristeas heard about a wintry region to the east, a place that sounded like one described in the legends of his homeland. Those legends told of a country whose entrance was a cave that housed Boreas, god of the north winds. The country was therefore called Hyperborea, or the Back of the North Wind.

At the border of this mountainous land, wrote Aristeas, lived the Arimaspians, a savage group of one-eyed people who eked out a living from the rocky soil and searched for gold in their rivers. But the gold was kept under strange guard:

In those mountains, griffins flourished. They could be seen in flight—enormous and wild, carrying whole oxen in their talons as they headed for their high-perched nests. The nests were lined with gold, which the griffins gathered and guarded jealously. Men from the puny

Golden as the ore they guarded, strong as lions, swift as hawks,
the mighty griffins of ancient times laired in lofty mountains and,
with their curving talons, slaughtered mortal treasure seekers.

one-eyed race that shared the mountains with the griffins sometimes climbed to their glittering aeries in search of treasure, but none succeeded, as far as was known.

Aristeas delivered all this information at Proconnesus and promptly vanished again, never to reappear. Some thought he might have returned to the wilds to view the griffins and perhaps make his own attempt to obtain some of their gold.

Elsewhere in the lands beyond Europe were other creatures as wondrous as the griffins. The Roc, a winged giant said to feed on the flesh of elephants, was sighted above coastal waters from Greece to China. Persia was home to the Simurg, which sometimes sheltered mortal children in its enormous nest.

These winged beasts, exotic and remote, could not fail to capture the human imagination. But they did not touch the heart and mind so deeply as the familiar birds that lived freely in human settlements and breathed the breath of the oldest magic. Every place where mortals dwelled, they heard the songs of birds — the liquid trill of the nightingale, the sparkling chatter of the wren, the plaintive cooing of the dove and the harsh cries of the raven. And in those tones, human listeners could detect the voices of the gods. With their gift of flight, birds essayed regions humans could not see and where they could never go. The birds' ease in the sky and ready access to the whole surface of the planet seemed evidence of divine powers. In early times birds were worshipped as manifestations of gods; and even in later centuries, when they were no longer so honored, some-

thing of the old magic still clung to them.

The signs of power were particularly evident in the family Corvidae — ravens and their smaller relatives, the crows. Black of feather, sharp of eye, harsh of voice, they were everywhere known as messengers of darkness. In Greece, it was said, ravens were storm bringers, and indeed, when the ebony wings flapped high in a darkening sky, the birds appeared to be dragging thunderclouds with them.

In Britain, and especially in Ireland, ravens were the birds of the war goddesses, Badb, Macha and Neman, collectively known as the Morrigan or, sometimes, *an badb catha* — meaning "the battle crow." It was they who screamed the death song high above fields where warriors fought; it was they who waddled and hopped in ungainly fashion among the dead and dying, plucking out the warriors' eyes and feeding on their still-warm flesh. In Wales, it was said, ravens formed an army under a medieval lord called Owein, son of Urien. At his signal, the birds would turn eagerly upon enemy warriors, attacking them from the air and ripping their flesh to shreds.

Ravens were birds of prophecy, too, appearing before warriors doomed to die in battle and flying in ominous pairs over houses soon to be visited by death. Their insight into the future was the source of the Irish phrase "ravens' knowledge," meaning the ability to see and know everything. And belief in the birds' power seemed almost universal: In Denmark, the appearance of a raven in a village portended the imminent death of the parish priest; in Wales, a visitor whose approach to a house was (continued on page 79)

JAPAN'S WINGED WAR MASTERS

In far Japan once dwelled the Tengu – a race of winged gnomes revered for their mastery of the martial arts and of the warrior's spirit. Their home was a fortress on Mount Kurama, north of Kyoto, but they themselves seemed to exist outside earthly time, and their kingdom was shrouded in mists. For a mortal to walk among these creatures was a blessing: Under their tutelage, mortals could absorb some of their power.

One who did so was Ushiwaka, son of Yoshitomo and a member of a powerful clan that lived during the turbulent era of the samurai wars. The father was killed, his clan's territory conquered, and the son banished to a distant monastery. In his desire

to avenge his father, Ushiwaka willed himself into the world of the Tengu. Each night, never knowing whether he waked or slept, he left the monastery and journeyed to the pavilions of the winged tribe. The Tengu welcomed Ushiwaka royally and instructed him in their arts. He watched the soldiers balance on slack ropes, their wings barely trembling. This exercise, explained the Tengu, was a corporeal manifestation of spiritual grace. Ushiwaka attempted it himself, and although he fell many times, he finally mastered the challenge of the rope.

But Ushiwaka would need more than spiritual strength if he was to fulfill his mission of vengeance, for his enemies were powerful. The Tengu therefore patiently schooled him in battle, in the use of the claw-headed pike and the wielding of the sword. The training was arduous, but in time Ushiwaka's blade glittered and sang with more than mortal power. He had learned to command it from the very center of his being.

Ushiwaka now was almost ready, but there remained one more preparatory step. He wished to see his father's shade where it dwelled in paradise. This, too, the Tengu

granted, but indirectly, as was their custom: They insisted that he must know the darkness before he could comprehend the light. Therefore, on wings of cloud, the Tengu King took the mortal to the place where the damned suffered. Ushiwaka saw a land where pale women drowned forever in a pond of blood; he saw a realm of hungry ghosts; he saw a hell where the weak forever burned. Scores of hells he saw, and Ushiwaka did not flinch: The fortitude of the Tengu burned in him. He journeyed on to paradise and received his father's blessing on the task ahead.

After that, Ushiwaka was irresistible. He conquered his father's enemies and regained his clan's territories. And throughout Ushiwaka's life, the Tengu King, winged and benevolent, remained his mentor.

heralded by the croaking of a raven was thought to be treacherous.

Such were the ravens' powers of prognostication, in fact, that the Irish domesticated individual birds and carefully recorded the meaning of their behavior: If a house raven called from the northeast end of the dwelling, thieves were in the stable; if it called from the master's bed before he left on a journey, he would not return safely; if it perched on a woman's pillow and cawed, that woman would soon die; if it spoke in a small, chuckling voice, sickness was coming to the family or to the cattle. If a man set off from home on a journey and his wife, watching from the doorstep, saw a raven flying ahead of his path, she knew she would soon be a widow.

The raven never lost its mantle of evil. Even in later centuries, when its presence on the battlefield was accepted as the natural action of a carrion-eater and its prophetic powers were given little credence by most people, the bird was feared. It was said, for example, that the raven was particularly partial to human flesh. For many years, a tale about this ghoulish appetite circulated throughout England and Scotland. It told of a medieval traveler who walked along a sunny lane one summer afternoon. He stopped to rest in the shade of an oak, throwing his sack and staff aside and leaning his back against the rough bark. The day was warm, and the traveler slipped toward sleep. He snapped to attention, however, when he heard hoarse voices in the leaves above his head.

"How shall we break our fast?" said one.

"I will tell you," was the answer. "Down in yonder green field a knight lies dead. His hound and his hawk have deserted him, and he is all alone. Sit on his neck and gnaw; I shall pluck out his bonny blue eyes. And when we are finished with him, no one will know he ever existed, except the wind, howling through the cage of his white bones."

Unnerved, the traveler jumped to his feet and stared up into the tree branches, to meet only the unwinking gaze of two sooty ravens who perched there. The ravens took flight. But the traveler, who left the place immediately, anxiously staring around as he walked, heard their harsh laughter echoing among the trees along his path.

Another incident involving ravens occurred in 17th Century Scotland. The scene was the little village of Halmadry in Sutherland, a place whose people were devoted to the rigorous practices of the Church of Scotland. The villagers gathered regularly to pray at the cottage of a certain man whose name has been lost—probably because the people of the region were extremely reluctant to discuss details of the episode.

From what little the villagers said, it seems that one autumn evening at twilight, when the prayer meeting should have ended, it did not. No one emerged from the cottage. After some time a neighbor noticed the eerie stillness that surrounded the place and looked in a window. The light in the cottage was dim, but she nevertheless saw the tableau inside with perfect clarity.

The woman's God-fearing neighbors

were not standing to recite their prayers, as was the custom. Instead, they knelt in a swaying row, men, women and a child, the householder's young son. Their faces were ashen; their unblinking eyes were turned toward a column that stood at the end of the room near the fireplace. On top of the column was perched a raven, hunchbacked, black as night, and possessed of a malevolent power so great that the woman at the window could feel its force even through the pane. The cottage, she later said, seemed to stink of evil.

She rapped at the casement; the people within made no response, but the bird turned its head so that one eye gleamed in her direction. At the sight of it, she gave a scream so terrible that some men who were walking down the village lane — farmers returning from nearby fields — ran to her aid. They clustered around her while she gasped out the story. Then they peered through the window at the householder and his company.

"This is devilry — or foolishness," said one man grimly. He kicked the door of the cottage open and strode inside.

Those at the window watched him walk toward the column where the raven perched. The bird turned its head toward him, and the man's face instantly whitened. He clenched his fists and opened his mouth to speak, but no sound issued forth. As if forced by an inexorable, invisible hand, the man sank to his knees and bowed his head to the bird.

After that, no one had the courage to enter the cottage. The villagers gathered in the yard and kept vigil through the night, anxiously whispering among themselves and peering through the windowpane. From time to time, they called out the names of their friends in the cottage and banged on the door, but the scene within never changed: All who had gone to the cottage to pray to God instead knelt in a swaying row and soundlessly worshipped the raven.

The vigil went on all through that long night and the next day and the next night. Inside the cottage, power throbbed and swelled; outside, the villagers of Halmadry prayed and talked. They would not venture into that heart of darkness. But

An avian familiar of death

Among birds that had powers of foretelling, the swan-necked Caladrius was thought to be the most noble: It was kept in great courts and heralded the deaths of kings. Scholars said the bird would turn its back on a sufferer who was soon to die. If a sick man had a chance at life, however, the bird magically absorbed his illness and flew away toward the sun, so that the mortal's malaise was dispersed harmlessly in the air.

80

they were good people, determined to find a way to release their fellows. On the morning of the third day, they decided to try fighting darkness with light.

The villagers placed ladders against the four sides of the house and, working as swiftly as they could, stripped away the musty reeds of the thatched roof, exposing the ridge tree and the rafters. Shafts of sunlight poured through the openings they made. Suddenly a hoarse shriek sounded, and black wings beat against the face of one of the workers. No one saw the raven fly away; the man himself, when he descended trembling to the ground, said he had seen only blackness and felt only a shudder as the evil thing passed by him. The raven had simply vanished.

The worshippers, freed from whatever spell had kept them in thrall, trailed slowly from the ruined cottage. The villagers clustered around, but they held back their questions when they saw the prisoners' faces. The cottage householder gripped his son by the shoulders and spoke for all of them.

"It was an old god who held us," he said. "He commanded that we sacrifice my boy to him. And he would have broken our will in time." Then he began to weep.

Who the raven spirit was or how it appeared in a civilized time to bend mortal will to its savage desires are things beyond knowing. Even among themselves, the villagers of Halmadry did not speculate on these matters. They wanted no reminder of the utter helplessness they had felt in that dim cottage.

Ravens, such as the one that haunted Halmadry, were not the only birds associated with evil; nor was the raven the only prophetic bird. For example, the owl—a predator that flew in darkness on silent wings—was considered a bird of such ill omen by Romans that buildings it entered required ritual cleansing. In Scotland the owl was called *cailleach oidhche*, or "night hag," and in Wales *aderyn y corff*, or "corpse bird." Its hooting presaged death. Yet the owl's power could be put to use if the bird was killed first. Farmers in Britain believed that they could avert hail and lightning by nailing an owl's body to a barn door with the wings outstretched.

The cuckoo, herald of spring, was believed to fly to the land of the dead in winter, and if it was heard calling from the north—where the land of the dead was said to be—it announced bad fortune. But a cuckoo calling from the south announced good harvest; from the east, luck in love; and from the west, general well-being. The Welsh said that folk traveling in search of fortune and adventure had only to follow the direction of a singing cuckoo's flight to find their heart's desire.

Some birds were almost wholly filled with goodness. Among them, the industrious wren, tiny but bright-voiced, was preeminent. It became the center of a ritual practiced for centuries throughout France and Britain.

Every December at about the time the winter-shortened days began to lengthen again (December 26, Saint Stephen's Day, was the date chosen in the Christian era), young men in rural villages went hunting the little bird. They killed

the first one they found— and the killer was made king for the day and given a robe and crown to wear. Then they placed its body on a pole and paraded through the village streets, singing a special wren song to greet the changing season. In some places the bird was buried in the churchyard after the ceremonies were finished. The purpose of the rite was to chase the winter darkness away. Perhaps the wren was chosen for this role because it was itself a frequenter of dark places; it made its nest in holes, crevices and dense thickets (thus its Latin name, *troglodytes troglodytes*, or "dweller in caves"). More likely, however, the bird was sacrificed as a particularly precious being, an enemy of cold and dark and death: The wren, it was said, brought fire—and therefore warmth and light—from heaven. Storytellers said that the wren once flew to the very source of light, the sun, and was set aflame— which accounts for the ruddy plumage the little bird wears in the spring.

It was also said that the robin, which is often found with the wren, flew too close during the smaller bird's heroic return from the sun and scorched its own feathers; hence the scarlet breast of the robin. Christians, however, said that the robin had attempted to stanch the blood that flowed from Christ's side during the Crucifixion and thus its feathers had been incarnadined. Whether touched by fire or by sacred blood, the bright-breasted bird, comfortably and cheerfully settled among the fields and cottages of its human neighbors, bore a mantle of sanctity. Hunters did not pursue it, and not even the naughtiest children ever attempted to rob its nest.

Over the millennia, many birds have been linked to the sun; they alone could ascend into the skies and withstand the heat and brilliance of the lamp of heaven. Fittingly, one of the most revered birds was said to be born and reborn of fire.

This was the Phoenix of Arabia and Egypt, a creature of unparalleled splendor. It was larger than an eagle; its head was golden, and in its iridescent feathers gleamed every color to be seen in flame— scarlet and lavender and gold and blue. It was the only creature of its kind, and it was variously believed to live three hundred, five hundred, or a thousand years. As its life neared the end, the Phoenix retreated to the highest fronds of a palm tree in the Arabian desert and, during a single night, built a nest of the most fragrant gums and spices—frankincense, cinnamon and myrrh among them. And when the first frail glow of the desert dawn gathered in the east, the magnificent bird sang the sun into flight, sang steadily while the golden

Enthroned on a nest of burning spices, the Phoenix of Arabia
sang its death song to the sun, then was reborn from its own ashes.

. . . With the aid of the Firebird, the Russian Princess found the sorceress who had
enchanted her land—and rescued her lover's heart from the fire that threatened it.

in the gardens of the palace, a bird caroled to greet the dawn.

The lovers had only a day together. Late in the afternoon, when darkness—natural darkness—made shadows in the garden, the young man fell. Caught in mid-sentence, he whitened, trembled, gasped once and dropped to the ground, where he lay still and pale as the dead.

The Princess long wept over him, then wandered distraught through the palace, stumbling against objects in the blackness, but caring nothing of pain. The courtyard seemed to call her back to her death-sleep, but before she lay on the bier of flowers, a gleam caught her eye. It was the Firebird's feather. She picked it up and warmed her hands on it.

After a time, wings flamed overhead, and the palace again filled with the Firebird's brilliance: The great bird had been summoned by the Princess's hand on its feather. It alighted near her and, with an inclination of its head, indicated dumbly that she should mount.

As soon as the Princess had nestled among the warm feathers, she was aloft. The bird took her high, beating steadily through the night sky in its own envelope of radiance. Such was the dazzle that the Princess saw neither the stars above nor the land far below. Then she felt the wings slow their beating. The ground became visible and lifted up to them, a desolate landscape of scarps and canyons and boulder-strewn hillsides. The Firebird settled at the foot of a cliff, and the shadows that had been flung crazily across the rocky terrain by its flight now grew still. Then the bird bent its head toward an opening in the cliff—a cave.

The Princess peered in and saw that it was occupied. A gaunt woman, robed in black, was chanting incantations over a fire that seemed not to be a fire but a smoky heap of blackened ice. A bubbling caldron rested on it.

As the Princess stared at the woman and her vessel, memories began to stir. She recalled herself as a girl in the palace, playing in halls that were filled with sunlight by day and that shimmered with firelight and candle flame by night. She recalled a dark sister who roamed those same halls, but who favored shadow and gloom. She recalled the sister's air of deepening hatred and the hours her sister spent studying dusty tomes and acquiring the lore of strange women and bleak-featured men who had somehow learned of her interests. She recalled the day that the sister gave herself to darkness, to become a night hag and cast the spell of sleep on the land. This was the author of her grief.

The Princess acted at once and without thought. She ran into the cavern and kicked the caldron from the fire. From the splashing liquid sprang a ruby jewel, shaped in the form of a heart. The Princess caught and clasped it in her hands. (Some storytellers said that the object was a living heart.) At this, the night witch screamed once, then vanished.

Outside the cavern, the Firebird still waited. She settled between its wings once again, holding in her hand the ruby heart that the witch had used to cast a spell upon her lover.

So the sun-bird's tale had a happy ending: The maiden found her Prince alive; she wed him, and high over their heads on their wedding day, the Firebird soared and tumbled, like a star or lesser sun.

A tale for children, some would say. Yet beneath its childish images rests a recollection of deeper powers. A land lay sterile, trapped in darkness, and the woman who should have ruled it slept as if unborn. Only a mortal could rescue her and restore life to her land, but a mortal alone could not press back the dark. That required the aid of an avatar of the light, a dazzling creature that sailed the sky on mighty wings, bearing the life-giving fire of the heavens, and watched with care the small workings of mortals' lives. ༒

An Enchanted Bestiary

From ancient times forward, many scholars told of
strange and wonderful creatures they had seen in the
course of their travels or had learned of at second
hand. In a world that had been imperfectly charted,
false tales sometimes flourished. For example, an
account of geese that hatched from barnacles was simply a mistaken explanation circulated by people
who had never seen the migratory birds nesting. (As a
result, the French word *canard*–duck–became a syn-
onym for a false report.) But that true marvels shared
the planet with mortals, no mortal could doubt.

The manticore and mermecolion

Among the leonine race were two oddities, one terrible, one piteous. In India lived the manticore, which had a lion's body, a manlike head, and an appetite for humans. No hunter was safe from the poisoned barbs of its tail or its triple rows of teeth. The gentle mermecolion of Asia, on the other hand, had a sorry make-up: a lion's head and the body of an enormous ant. Because the ant's digestive system could not tolerate the meat the lion head craved, the wretched creature always died within a few hours of birth.

The vegetable lamb

Venturesome travelers to the realm of the Tartars,
on the shores of the Caspian Sea, reported sightings
of small, woolly beasts that popped from the ripen-
ing gourds of certain trees. Valued for its warm wool,
the *barometz*—or "little lamb," in the Tartar tongue—
had a short, cruel life. The *barometz* remained
rooted by an umbilical cord to its pod, feeding on the
grasses that surrounded its tree. When no grass remained within its reach, the lamb died.

The basilisk

Deadliest of serpents, this native of the empty Libyan deserts derived its name from the Greek *basileus*, or "king," because it was the monarch of its kind. In its brightly colored cock's head burned enormous eyes, whose baleful glance could kill. Its very breath brought pestilence to the regions it inhabited and was said to kill even the birds that flew in the sky above. Although its body was serpentine, the basilisk moved not by slithering on its belly but in rearing coils.

The catoblepas and gulon

Great appetite characterized some ancient beasts: In Ethiopia lived the catoblepas, a scaly, buffalo-like animal said to gnaw on its own forelegs. Its heavy head nodded continually; hence its name, which in Greek meant, "that which looks downward." This circumstance was fortunate, for the sluggish animal's glance, like the basilisk's, could kill. Far to the north, in the Scandinavian snow fields, hunters pursued the *gulon*, a gluttonous carrion-feeder whose fur had a mottled, damask quality prized in hatmaking.

The peryton

A powerful flier, the deerlike *peryton* may perhaps have been related to the winged Pegasus of Greece. According to early writers, the beast had one unique characteristic: The shadow it cast was that of a man, which led scholars to believe that *perytons* were the spirits of wayfarers who had died far from home. The creatures were sighted frequently in Classical times over Mediterranean islands and near the Strait of Gibraltar. They were thought to be man-eaters, swooping in flocks upon unsuspecting sailors and devouring them; no weapon could avail against the strength of the *perytons*.

Chapter Three

Paragon of Purity

Tapestry makers of times gone by expended endless hours attempting to capture the unicorn in cloth. First, designers painted the beast on huge rectangles of linen, lingering over the unicorn's shining whiteness and single spiraling horn; they posed it in fields spangled with a thousand flowers and threaded with silver streams. Then, on massive, upright wooden looms, the skilled weavers of Bruges and Brussels and Lille copied the designers' paintings (called cartoons) with threads of the finest wool and silk, dyed red with madder and blue with woad, or coated with beaten silver and gold. In the end, when the clicking bobbins at last fell silent and the final threads were tied off, the weavers had treasure to offer: enchanting tapestries fit to grace the walls of the finest of palaces and please the eyes of idle courtiers.

They were wonders, indeed, those woven images. They showed the unicorn at peace in its forest and at battle with men. Yet the tapestries were no more than mortal makings; they gave only faint echoes of the unicorn's nobility and mysterious power. After all, these designers, these spinners of wool, these dyers and these weavers in their workshops and guildhalls were townsmen and indoor people, who rarely thought to venture beyond the sheltering walls of their settlements into the wild world that lay beyond. None of them had ever seen the living unicorn, which dwelled in mountain fastnesses or in forests remote from the bustling towns.

Only adventurers might find unicorns, and adventurers were not sedentary craftsmen. They were hunters, men who sought to capture the wild creature and turn its magic to their own uses. Here is the tale of one of their hunts:

It took place in France, perhaps in Anjou, but more probably in Brittany, near the forest of Brocéliande, where creatures like unicorns could still live. Old magic was strong in Brocéliande, breathing among the huge oaks and in thick underbrush. The very borders of the place seemed to shift about in the silvery light and trailing mists of the Breton hills. And although scattered castles and even unfortified villages had begun to appear near the verge of that wood, few humans ventured into the tangled dimness.

101

No charcoal burners' fires smoked beneath the leafy canopy. No poachers crept among the trees: Even the fattest hare was not worth the risk of meeting with the ghosts and fairies and ancient gods said to dwell in Brocéliande. The place seemed safe from mortals.

One frosty autumn morning, however, a man walked slowly along the edge of the haunted wood, peering about him with sharp, well-trained eyes. He wore a red jerkin for warmth and thick leggings to protect him against thorns and brambles; a curving hollow ox horn chased with silver hung by a strap from his shoulder. Beside him, straining at the stout leash he held, paced a heavy-set hound, its nose close to the ground, its long ears swaying as its head swung from side to side.

The man was a lymerer, one of the huntsmen of a Breton lord whose name has been lost. His task that morning was the first step in the stately ritual of the medieval hunt: With his lymer, or bloodhound, he had been assigned to find and track a stag to its lair and mark its position so that the lord and the lord's hunting party could pursue it. On this morning, however, the lymerer found something that surpassed even the most royal of stags.

He found it suddenly, between one step and the next. He froze where he stood, staring; the dog, too, paused motionless. A unicorn loomed before them in the gloom of the wood, a pale shadow against the black columns of the tree trunks. The beast's muscles swelled smoothly under a coat as white as moonlight; the spiraling horn — worth many times its weight in gold — shone like pearl. For a moment, the unicorn's dark and liquid eyes remained fastened upon the intruding man and his dog. Then the creature turned and trotted back into the forest of Brocéliande. Its hoofs made no sound in the morning quiet.

An expert at his craft, the lymerer did nothing to startle the beast. He made neither sound nor move until after the unicorn had vanished among the trees. Then he carefully noted his position and devised an arrangement of twigs to indicate the direction the quarry had taken. Afterward, with his dog panting beside him, he made off across the stubbled fields, toward the distant towers of his master's fortress.

Within two hours, the lymerer returned to the verge of the forest, and this time he was not alone. He led a glittering procession. In plumed hats and brocaded doublets, in velvets and silk, the lord with his courtiers and his lady with her maidens rode toward the wood, the bells on their bridles ringing clear in the chill air. The courtiers were armed with swords. All around them flocked the crowd of men and animals that formed the company of the hunt — bowmen and spear bearers, grooms and pages and, riding alone, the leatherclad master of the hunt, a harassed-looking man who already had his horn in his hand. He snapped a steady stream of orders to those in his charge.

Behind the master, walking amid a living sea of sleek bodies and wagging tails, came the two keepers of the hounds, each holding dozens of leashes. One of these

men controlled a pack of velvet-collared greyhounds, which hunted by sight; the other commanded the running hounds, or coursers, which hunted by scent. There were sixty animals in all, and they were yoked together in pairs, with couplings woven from sturdy horsehair.

As this company neared the forest, the master of the hunt raised his hand, and the riders drew to a halt. He bent from his saddle to confer with the lymerer.

"You saw the beast here?" he said.

"Aye."

"This is the forest of Brocéliande. No man dares to go there, they say."

The lymerer shrugged. "It was a unicorn," he said. "I saw the horn."

The master glanced at his lord, who nodded, eyes alive with interest and avarice. Then, at a signal from the huntsman, the keeper of the running hounds released two of his dogs. These, with the lymerer and his hound, plunged at once into the forest, searching for the track that led to the unicorn's lair. Distant baying told the waiting company when the scent had been picked up. The noise was followed swiftly by the high note of the lymerer's horn, and

Deep in a forest in France, hunters found a unicorn in a flowering grove. They prodded it from its lair with spears so that they might have the pleasure of the chase. In the end, they slew the magic beast to gain the treasure of its horn.

Such was the pride and ferocity of unicorns that they could not be taken alive. Yet
mortals—more prideful still—liked to think that they might hold the beautiful
beast captive, and so they wove tapestry prisons to contain the unicorn's image.

the hunters sprang into action. The keepers loosed both greyhounds and running hounds, and these set out along the forest track, followed by the lord, his huntsman and his courtiers. At the lord's orders, the women held back.

The riders had not far to go – a mile of forest, perhaps – before they found the lymerer. He waited at the edge of a clearing in the trees, and he had leashed the hounds. He gestured toward the clearing. What the company saw there brought absolute silence. Even the most excitable of the hounds quieted.

In the lord's own lands, autumn held sway; the fields were brown, and leaves fluttered from the trees, gathering in drifts of dun and scarlet and gold. In the clearing of Brocéliande, however, all was in bloom. Fragrant with blossom and at the same time heavy with fruit, orange trees grew there, and peach and medlar and apricot as well. A clear stream bubbled through this grove, and it was edged with flowers and herbs – blue forget-me-nots and healing feverfew and plantain. Birds sang amid the blossoms and fruit trees. They did not fly off when they saw the huntsmen but quickly clustered in the shielding shadow of a white unicorn, which stood as still as if carved in ivory.

Earth had not anything to show more fair. The unicorn's steady gaze, both fierce and fearless, was bent upon the encroaching mortals and their dogs.

"We cannot kill this beast," said the lymerer softly. His greed had left him.

But the master huntsman replied in quite another tone, breaking the spell that held the hunters.

"Not now," he said. "There is no sport in that." He looked around for the lord's approval, and received it. As in stag hunting, the prey should not be killed in its lair. It had to be started from safety – "unharbored" was the technical term – and sent fleeing in terror before the pack and the huntsmen in order to give hunters the pleasure of a fine chase. If all went as planned and the beast was young and strong, the hunters could count on two hours of bruising riding before they brought the exhausted quarry down.

The master of the hunt therefore gave the signal to coerce the unicorn into flight. The hounds surged forward, snarling, with the spearmen right behind. At once, the birds took wing, swerving up and away among the trees. The unicorn at first held its ground, but when men and hounds closed in, it reared. Pandemonium broke loose. Spearmen circled, shouting, just out of range of the slashing hoofs. The lead hounds fell back, yelping, but one greyhound was too slow. The unicorn pierced the dog's flank with a sudden thrust of its horn and tossed its victim into the air. The greyhound fell twitching among its fellows.

At that instant, a spear found its mark in the unicorn's shoulder, and blood streaked down the white side. Whirling, the unicorn drove back the circle of tormentors. Then it sprang high and, in three great leaps, fled the clearing and vanished among the trees.

The master huntsman blew the *appel*, a deep, trembling note signifying that the

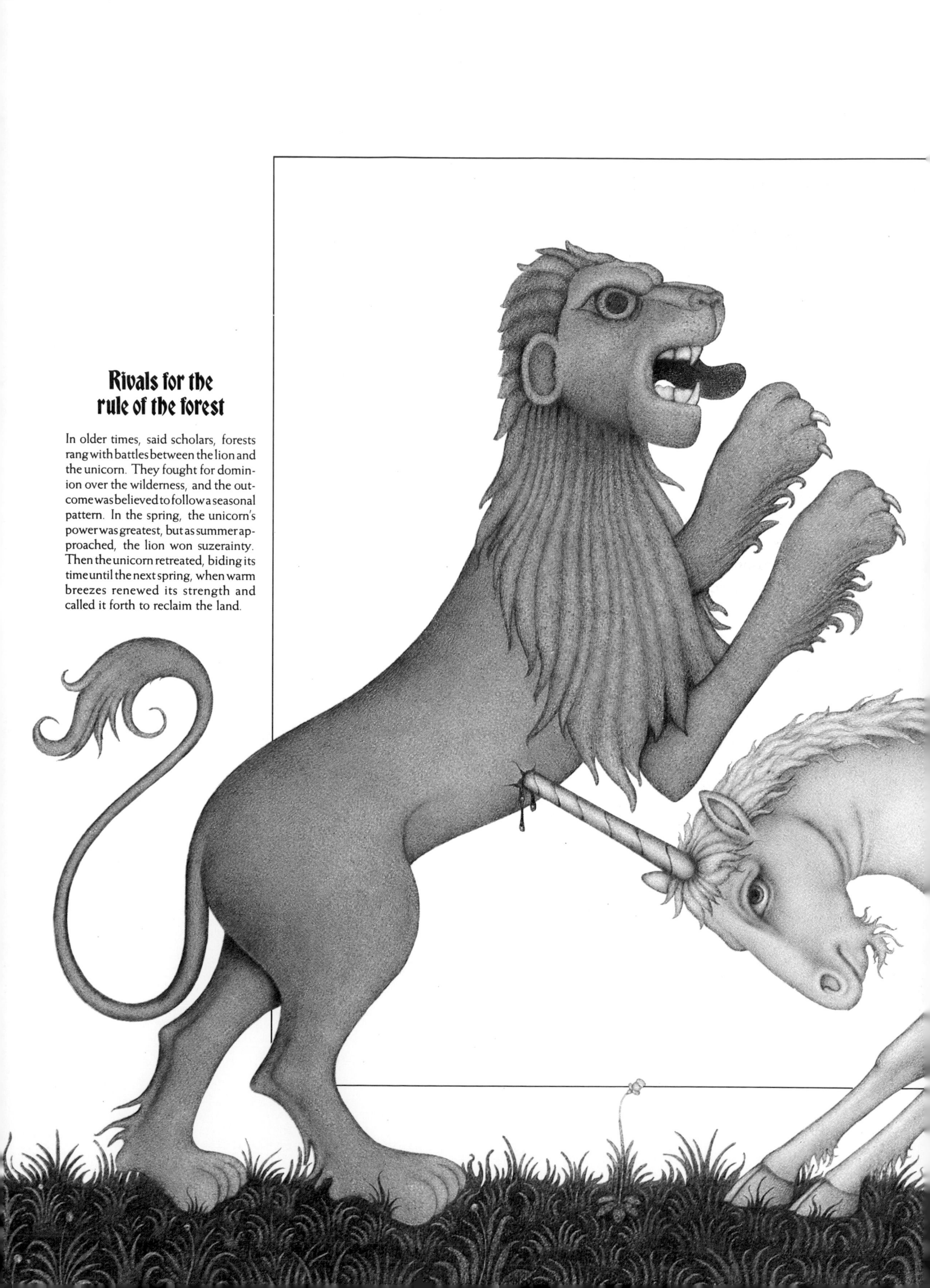

Rivals for the rule of the forest

In older times, said scholars, forests rang with battles between the lion and the unicorn. They fought for dominion over the wilderness, and the outcome was believed to follow a seasonal pattern. In the spring, the unicorn's power was greatest, but as summer approached, the lion won suzerainty. Then the unicorn retreated, biding its time until the next spring, when warm breezes renewed its strength and called it forth to reclaim the land.

quarry had been unharbored. The hounds hurtled into the trees on the unicorn's trail. Behind galloped the master of the hunt, and the company followed him.

Only the lord paused. A scholarly man as well as a hunter, he knew what his master huntsman did not. This rarest of creatures might provide the same chase as a common stag, but it was no simple beast of nature, and unless special measures were taken, it would not die at human hands when its strength flagged. Only in the presence of a maiden would the unicorn surrender. The lord therefore ordered a young page of the company to carry instructions to his lady; then he too joined the hunting pack.

Denied the pleasure of the chase, the boy sighed and turned back. He found the women easily enough. They had remained at the edge of the wood, strolling about with their long, scalloped sleeves trailing in the grass. Robed as they were in crimson and blue, their looped braids crowned with gold nets, they made a bright picture — as though birds of paradise had settled in the autumn fields. The page dismounted and gave his lord's message.

His lady nodded, regarding him thoughtfully. Then she smiled and said, "Never mind, boy. You can follow the chase by the music today."

And indeed, this was true. The forest rang with the varied signals of the hunting horns, the gutteral baying of the hounds and the barks of the greyhounds. In those days, the song of a hunting pack in full cry stirred such deep feelings that Gace de la Buigne, the French King's own chaplain, was moved to write: "When the hounds

A double-horned curiosity

Southern India was the home of a curious creature that appeared to be a distant relative of the unicorn of the West. It was called the *eale* or *yale*. Its head was bearded, goat-fashion, as were the heads of many unicorns, and it bore spiraling horns. Evidently, the horns could be swiveled in different directions for maximum effectiveness in battle. The Indians kept these beasts in temples, it was said, as guardians against evil spirits.

give tongue, never has man heard melody to equal this. No Alleluia sung in the chapel of the King is so beautiful."

Now close and loud, now receding into the depths of the wood, so that even the horn calls were faint, the hunting music went on and on. The page strode about in an agony of frustration, but the court women murmured among themselves, talking on timeworn topics; they were used to waiting. The lady read from a tiny Book of Hours that hung by a chain from her jeweled belt. Periodically she raised her head and listened. After more than an hour had passed, she closed her book.

"They are driving the quarry toward this open ground," she said. "It cannot be killed in Brocéliande. Come, my dear." And following the order that the page had brought, she took the hand of a fair-haired child, the youngest of her maidens, and led the girl forward. The rest of her companions scattered toward their horses, to be out of the path of the hunt. The lady guided the girl to a spot near the dark line

of the forest trees and indicated that she should stand there. Then she, too, mounted and rode a little distance away.

The maiden waited, her back straight, her hands clasped at her waist. Her head trembled, but she held her place while the noise of the hunt thundered toward her through the wood.

Suddenly branches crashed and the unicorn sprang from the trees, heading straight toward the maiden. Its flanks heaved piteously, and blood trickled from its nostrils. But even then, hunted thing that it was, it shone with lunar beauty.

A moment of eerie stillness followed. The shapes of the huntsmen and horses and hounds flickered among the trees behind the unicorn. But the great beast did not move. It had seen the maiden.

Then, as if it knew its hour had come, it stepped forward, calm now. It sank to its knees before the girl, leaned its ivory-crowned head gently against her side and gave itself up to its fate.

Death came in an instant. The lord

rode forward and lifted the maiden out of harm's way, and the hounds burst from the wood, lunging at the unicorn and tearing its flesh with bared teeth. Close behind the hounds were the spearmen, screaming curses from twisted faces as they plunged their blades into throat and heart. Blood spurted; the unicorn jerked and was still.

Then the master of the hunt raised his horn to his lips. Up into the heavens sailed the high notes of the mort—the formal music of a successful kill. The horn song was the call of human triumph. That bloodthirsty cleric de la Buigne wrote of it: "No man who hears such melody would wish for any other."

Thus died beauty beyond mortal comprehension, a sacrifice to human pleasure. The rare beast was slung across a horse's back and taken to the lord's fortress, to be butchered according to the rules used for stags. Choice portions went to the lymerer and the master of the hunt for their work; the hounds fought over the entrails. The ivory horn, which had magical qualities, went to the lord and his lady.

And all rested, well satisfied, undisturbed by the destruction of the unicorn. As that intrepid 14th Century huntsman, Gaston, Comte de Foix, surnamed Phoebus, wrote of the hunter at the end of the day: "Afterward, in the evening of the night, he takes the air because of the great heat that he has had and then he goes and drinks and lies down in his bed in fresh linen and sleeps well—all night long without any evil thoughts. Wherefore I say that hunters go to paradise when they die and live in this world more joyfully than any other men."

The huntsmen lived in a time when unicorns were already strangers to humanity, elusive spirits that dwelled apart from mortals, preferring places where magic might still be found. Unicorns were more spoken of than seen. A thousand tales arose about their fleetness and nobility, about their horns' powers of detecting poison or purifying water, about the beasts' ability to escape death at mortal hands except in the presence of a maiden. In their efforts to discover the origin of these curious qualities, scholars searched diligently among the available Classical texts for references to unicorns—and found more baffling information than they had bargained for.

The first unicorn seen in Europe was described in a matter-of-fact way in Julius Caesar's account of his campaigns among the Celts, *The Gallic War*. He had heard tales that the creatures inhabited the Hercynian forest near the Rhine—a stretch of woods so deep that even a sixty days' journey would not take a man from one edge to the other. It seemed the perfect place for a beast as shy as the unicorn; and indeed Caesar reported a sighting of one "shaped like a stag, from the middle of whose forehead, between the ears, stands forth a single horn, taller and straighter than the horns we know." But that was all he recorded—a soldier's dry comment on a brief vision of a wonder.

For more than sightings, it was necessary to go farther back in time and farther eastward. From the information that surfaced, it appeared that the continent of

Among the swarm of humankind, the unicorn acknowledged the mastery only of maidens pure and fair. In the presence of such a paragon, the beast lost its wildness and paid homage.

Asia had given birth to the unicorn, or at least to its ancestors.

An early mention of the unicorn's existence came from a Greek named Ctesias of Cnidus, who served as a physician to the Persian Kings Artaxerxes II and Darius II, around the end of the Fifth Century B.C. In the courts of these monarchs, Ctesias heard of many curiosities, and he took care to report them to his countrymen.

"There are in India," Ctesias wrote, "certain wild asses that are as large as horses and even larger. Their bodies are white, their heads dark red, and their eyes dark blue. They have a horn in the middle of the forehead that is one cubit [about eighteen inches] in length. The base of this horn is pure white. The upper part is sharp and of a vivid crimson, and the middle portion is black. Those who drink from these horns, made into drinking vessels, are not subject, they say, either to convulsions or to the falling sickness. Indeed, they are immune even to poisons if, either before or after swallowing such, they drink wine, water, or anything else from these beakers."

Ctesias himself never saw the wildly colored creature he described. He simply repeated tales that travelers to the Himalayas and Tibet—regions included in the then-vague appellation "India"—had told him. It may be that he heard garbled stories of the unicorn of China, which was revered above all other creatures and considered king of the beasts that lived on land.

This unicorn was known as the k'i-lin: K'i was the male of the type, lin the female. It had a stag's body, although its hoofs were those of a horse, and the horn it bore was twelve feet long. Its body colors were as various as the bands of the rainbow. The k'i-lin was no savage beast of the forest to be savagely hunted: It was comparable in power and wisdom to the dragon, and it appeared to mortals only at rare intervals as a bearer of great tidings.

The first time it was seen, according to the chroniclers, was in 2697 B.C. Resplendent in its many-colored coat, the k'i-lin appeared from nowhere and silently trod the halls and pavilions of the Emperor Huang-ti before vanishing again. By that sign, the people knew that the years of his reign would be full of felicity. As indeed they were: Huang-ti was said to have invented musical instruments and taught his people how to build with bricks; it was he who first unified the Chinese people. The k'i-lin appeared to Huang-ti once more, at the very end of his life, to bear him on its back to the world of the dead.

It was said, too, that the k'i-lin showed itself to a young woman named Yen Chen-tsai in a temple in the Sixth Century B.C. Lowering its massive head, the beast dropped a jade tablet into her hand. On the tablet were inscribed characters indicating that she would bear a son who would be a throneless king. And the son she later bore was the sage Confucius, a throneless king indeed: His teachings gave rise to the system of order and obedience that shaped Chinese thought and government for centuries.

The k'i-lin was invariably a benefactor. It could tell good from evil, the Chinese wrote; it ate no living thing; and its appearance preceded the birth of great men, such as Confucius. Images of the beast were affixed to the crimson chairs that traditionally carried Chinese brides to the homes of their new husbands and were pasted on the doors of the women's quarters in thousands of Asian homes to ensure auspicious births.

The Chinese unicorn walked so softly that its hoofs made no sound. It was as noble as the unicorns that ranged the European forests, but it lacked their fierceness, and Ctesias' tales may have derived not from descriptions of this creature but from garbled reports concerning a wolfish, single-horned beast that inhabited the plains of Persia and India. That creature was known variously as the *karg* or *karkadann*. A solitary predator, it was so ferocious that wild animals refused to graze anywhere within its territory. Its strength was such that it successfully attacked even elephants. The slaying of the beast was a star in any prince's crown.

Although singular in its aggressiveness, the *karkadann* shared two characteristics with the unicorns of Europe: It was said that the beast could be tamed by the presence of young women and that knife handles made from its horn exuded a kind of sweat, trembling violently in the presence of poison.

The first of these characteristics has never been satisfactorily explained, although scholars in Europe devoted endless investigation and speculation to the problem. Christians preferred to believe that the presence of a maiden acted on the creature as a balm: Faced with perfect mor-

The unicorn of China was a beast of the gods, rarely seen by men and women. Along with the Phoenix, it dwelled in the world beyond the clouds, where the great immortals forever feasted.

*The Chinese k'i-lin, herald of good fortune, appeared before the woman who was
to bear Confucius the philosopher. She sought to tether it by looping a silken
line around its horn, but the beast merely bowed and disappeared.*

The Asian unicorn, known in Japan as the kirin, possessed
an unerring sense of justice. Sometimes it appeared
in courts of law to slay the guilty and free the innocent.

tal purity, the unicorn, noblest beast of the elder world, fell to its knees in willing surrender. (A startling variant of this theory was proposed by the 12th Century German scholar and poet, the abbess Hildegard of Bingen. She wrote that the unicorn was overcome with love for women placed in its path. Finding them "enticing and delightful," the beast succumbed.)

Like called to like, it seemed. Pure and gentle in the wild, the unicorn bowed to purity and gentleness among mortals. And the unicorn in the wild, unthreatened by humans, was the very embodiment of serenity, a godlike protector of the animals around it. Medieval travelers fortunate enough to glimpse the creature told how, with magic, it cleansed lakes and rivers for the benefit of other animals. Johannes of Hese, a priest of Utrecht who visited the Holy Land in the 14th Century, wrote of a unicorn that performed this service at the bitter river Marah on the field of Helyon, in what is now the Sinai peninsula.

After sunset each day, Johannes said, the waters of the river Marah were poi-

soned by the venom of nocturnal creatures. But the waters were purified at dawn: "In the morning, after the sunrise, comes the unicorn and dips his horn into the stream, driving the poison from it so that the good animals can drink there during the day. This I have seen myself."

The unicorn also gave succor to mortals, as medieval tales attest. In his later years, for instance, King Arthur of Britain was fond of telling his knights the story of such a beneficent unicorn. It was one that he had encountered in his youth, at the beginning of his reign. The tale began when the King sailed a small boat into the seas off Scotland in search of adventure. It was well known that the little islands scat-

tered there harbored strange and savage beings, worthy to test a warrior's mettle.

One day the King found himself becalmed in a heavy fog. The little vessel drifted, its soaked sail flapping, until at last it grated onto a pebbly shore. The King sprang out, pulled the boat up onto the shingle and set off inland to find whatever might await him.

At first he saw no sign of habitation. Then a stone tower loomed ahead, standing stern and solitary among tall trees. The King contemplated the structure with perplexity for some moments: Its gray walls were blank, apparently unpierced by either door or window. His reverie was broken when a voice spoke close by.

"Hail, stranger," it said. "Who are you, and how can you be served?"

Arthur turned and saw an elderly, dwarfish man. The man was unarmed. From a seamed and leathery face, wise eyes regarded the King.

"I am Arthur of Britain, cast upon your shore and at your mercy," he replied.

"You shall have it," said the dwarf. "When the mist rises, I will send you safely on your way." He offered the King water to drink. When Arthur had drunk his fill, he asked, "Are you the only man here? How came you to this lonely place?"

"I am not alone," answered the dwarf. "I will gladly tell you the tale of my life, to pass the time."

So the two sat together on the grass, and the dwarf told his tale. He had been born in Northumberland, he said, and lived there happily until the capricious King of that province had exiled him, sending him with his pregnant wife to this far-off island. They were left on the shore, without weapons and without food. Shortly afterward, with only her husband to help her, the young woman gave birth to a son—and died. The dwarf wrapped the infant in his wife's cloak. He made a cairn of stones to cover her body and set off into the trees near the shore,

seeking shelter from the wind and rain.

He found shelter for the infant in a great oak. Its trunk had a hollow, he said, large enough for six knights to sleep in.

Within the hollow lay a marvel: three tiny white fawnlike creatures, their gangling legs curled under them. Their eyes were shut; they slept. Each had a small star of light in the center of its forehead — the beginning of a unicorn's horn.

The dwarf laid his child among them, along their warm flanks. Then he heard a sound and turned to face the mother. She was as large as a horse and as white as a cloud, and the spiraled horn that grew from her forehead had a tip that glittered like tempered steel. The unicorn struck the ground once with a forefoot. She lowered her head for the charge. The dwarf, terrified, slipped by her and fled, leaving behind the baby boy.

He did not run far, for he heard the infant's wails. Then they stopped abruptly. He crept back toward the oak and listened. No sound came from within. He peered into the dark hollow, and saw a gleam of white. The unicorn had lain down and was nursing his son.

Thus, said the dwarf, his life on the island began. For a time, the unicorn sheltered both him and his son. The boy grew

strong and large; he was a giant of a child, for he had been nourished on magic milk. Eventually, father and son built themselves their own shelter—first a hut of branches, then this stone tower—and so they lived contented, wrapped in the unicorn's magic, far from the cares of men. The unicorn, the dwarf said, guarded them always, as if they were her own.

His story ended; the dwarf fell silent. Arthur raised his brows and asked, "And where are the boy and the unicorn now?"

"Yonder," said the dwarf, gesturing.

And indeed they were. A hulking young man emerged from the thinning mist. Like his father, he had a weather-beaten face—the face of a man at peace. Across his shoulder was slung the carcass of a bear; he had been hunting meat for his father. And beside him, as silver as if made of the mist itself, stood the unicorn. A nimbus of light shone all around it and glowed on the young hunter's face. The beast was more beautiful, King Arthur later said, than anything he had ever seen, more beautiful than the clouds that raced across the winter moon, more beautiful than the morning star. The two mortals on the island—the dwarf and his son—were swathed in enchantment, and this was its source. Arthur bowed his head before the unicorn. Tears stood in his eyes: Much as he desired to, he knew he could not stay in this sweet place. He had many leagues to travel and deeds to do before he could rest. But the unicorn and its two humble companions had revealed to him what true peace and harmony were.

The King soon left the island. When the mist lifted and the wind freshened, the dwarf and his son took him to the shore. They told him how to navigate to reach the outer islands he sought, and they helped him put to sea again. As Arthur brought the little boat about and wind filled the sail, he looked back toward the island. The two men stood on the shingle, waving him on his way. And behind them, among the dark trees, a starlike glimmer showed where the unicorn stood.

King Arthur became his own legend; he himself was the soul of chivalry and, more than that, a font of generosity and kindness. He had looked upon a mystery and, for a moment, was bathed in its enchantment, but in his wisdom he had never sought to master it. He was unique among humankind.

Most mortals hunted the unicorn for the splendid sport it gave—and for its ivory horn, in which all the creature's grace and purity seemed centered.

The horn's efficacy was well known by Arthur's time, for scholars had the manuscripts of the Second Century Roman, Claudius Aelianus, called Aelian. This naturalist emulated Ctesias of Cnidus in his description of the unicorn of India, but he said that the animal's horn was spiraled, and he went on to state: "These variegated horns, I learn, are used as

drinking-cups by the Indians – although not, to be sure, by all of the people. Only the great men use them, after having them ringed about with hoops of gold exactly as they would put bracelets on some beautiful statue. And it is said that whosoever drinks from this kind of horn is safe from all incurable diseases, such as convulsions and the so-called holy disease [epilepsy], and that he cannot be killed by poison."

The account of Aelian and of writers who followed him in later centuries were of great and urgent interest: Murder by poison seems to have reached epidemic proportions in medieval courts. The practitioners of the art had a battery of venoms at hand. Among plants, aconitine – referred to as "the queen mother of poisons" – was a common toxin, easily obtained from such deceptively pretty flowers as monkshood or wolfsbane. Within moments of ingestion, aconitine produced a freezing sensation that crept outward from the core of the body; eventually paralysis stopped the workings of the victim's heart. Murderers also used hemlock, which induced a paralysis that slowly ascended from the feet to the head, and attacked the respiratory muscles, causing death. (One of its worse characteristics was that the sufferer's mind remained clear to the end.) Black hyoscyamus – or henbane – and thorn apple were used as well. They produced maniacal excitement, distorted vision and death.

Of elemental poisons, arsenic, found in many ores, was a favorite, although mercury and antimony sulfide also came into play. Each caused – in some cases almost instantly – violent vomiting and eventual circulatory or kidney failure in their victims. No less varied than the list of poisons were the means devised to administer them without throwing suspicion on the poisoner. Murderers placed their deadly compounds in the scented pomander balls that courtiers used to ward off bad smells, so that the victims died by inhalation. They manufactured jeweled rings and knives from which tiny, envenomed pins would spring into the flesh. They impregnated clothing with poison, so that it would be absorbed through the skin.

In the 14th Century, rumor had it that Spain's King John I of Castile died after wearing poisoned boots; and in the next century, it was said that Henry VI of England succumbed to poisoned gloves. French poisoners imbued shirts with a mixture of arsenic, cantharides (powders made from poisonous beetles), and other irritants. These, when worn, produced suppurating skin lesions that resembled syphilis. Sufferers from syphilis at that time were treated with mercury, which usually finished the job.

But the primary means of administering poison was in food or wine, and it is therefore unsurprising that the rich and noble were willing to pay thousands in gold coin for the protection of a unicorn's horn, which not only changed

A pair of Persian killers

With any Persian beast, a single horn was a sign of predatory habits. Savagery lurked well-hidden in the *shadhavar*, an antelope-like creature whose curving horn was fluted with hollow branches. When the wind sighed through these branches, they sounded plaintive notes so sweet that animals of the mountains drew near to listen – and were promptly slain by the summoner.

From an island in the Indian Ocean came the *mi'raj*, even more innocent in appearance. The creature was a large yellow hare adorned with a single black horn. But all other animals knew its ravenous nature and fled for their lives whenever it approached.

The taming voice of the ringdove

Despite the violence of its nature, the *karkadann* could be put in sweet temper by the gentle voice of the ringdove. It was said that the beast would lie for hours beneath desert trees in which the birds cooed, enraptured by their song. And if a ringdove happened to alight on its horn, the *karkadann* would remain motionless, so as not to disturb the bird until it chose to fly away.

color or produced drops of moisture in the presence of toxins but also prevented the poisons' effects.

Vessels made of the horn figured prominently in the inventories of almost all royal—and clerical—treasuries. Among the most famous was the horn, seven feet long and weighing thirteen pounds, kept at the abbey at Saint-Denis, outside Paris. The treasury of the Basilica of St. Mark in Venice had three celebrated horns, one of them mounted on a pedestal of silver, so that it resembled a candlestick.

In fact, the mountings for the horns usually were of preciousness that matched the horns themselves. In the 15th Cen-

tury, for instance, a Burgundian ambassador to the court of Edward IV of England was presented with a cup of gold that was garnished with pearl and had at its center a segment of unicorn horn seven inches long. And as late as the 16th Century, the eminent Florentine goldsmith Benvenuto Cellini was commissioned by Pope Clement VII to design a mounting for a magnificent horn in the Pope's possession.

The ebullient craftsman had never seen a unicorn, but he designed what he deemed to be a most accurate representation: a golden head, partly "in the form of a horse's head and partly in that of a hart's, adorned with the finest sort of wreaths and

124

other devices," into which the horn could be inserted. Another, less inspired design was preferred to Cellini's. Cellini attributed this to the fact that the horn was intended to be a gift from the Pope to the King of the French – "an undiscriminating, tasteless people." (Clement did indeed present the horn to Francis I and, thereby, apparently, lost its benefits: The Pope was said to have died after inhaling smoke from a poisoned processional torch.)

Even powder ground from *verum cornu monocerotis* – or "true unicorn's horn" – was worth ten times its weight in gold; an entire horn could bring twice that. Not surprisingly, considering the rarity of the animal, there flourished a brisk trade in false horns manufactured from the tusks of elephants or powder made from the bones of fossil animals.

But real horns, full of the virtue of the magical beast, came only from living animals, caught, as the unicorn of Brocéliande was caught, by human hunters, and betrayed into death by human guile.

One especially shameful killing of a unicorn occurred in Bulgaria several centuries ago. The place of the deed was a shabby hamlet – a collection of rickety wooden cottages flanking a single street. Beyond them lay fields that provided the villagers' monotonous diet of carrots, turnips, potatoes and barley. And beyond the fields stretched miles of dark and scented pine forest, thought by the villagers to be haunted by witches and demons.

For all its meanness, the hamlet was self-sufficient. The villagers had flocks of chickens, and they raised pigs, which lived well on human leavings and could be slaughtered in the autumn and salted down for the winter. The cottages were served by two wells – rare enough in those parts. The peasants shared a pair of oxen for plowing, and they had a mule.

They were a close and insular group. Few of them ventured far along the muddy track that led to the outside world, and intruders – the rare peddlers and pilgrims passing through – were coolly received and sent briskly on their way. A wooden church stood in the village, but at the time of this tale its priest had long since died. No new priest had come to the place, so the building was used for storing hay. It was later said that the villagers indulged in pagan rites of worship, although the evidence for this was no more than what might be found in any rural hamlet of the era: At harvesttime, the people made corn dollies – little images to propitiate the earth mother; they sacrificed small animals at the solstices; and they hung iron over their doors to keep bad spirits away.

The village might have gone on with little change for centuries – as unnoticed as other places of its kind, sunk in the placid routine of plowing, sowing and reaping – except that disaster struck. The wells went bad. Their water turned brackish in a single night. Algae began to shine on the water's surface and crawl along the wooden well walls. The villagers blamed this misfortune on a peddler who had passed through weeks before, and they became more withdrawn than ever. They took water from a less convenient source: Each day, laden with buckets slung on car-

When a Bulgarian maiden led a unicorn to her village
to cleanse the wells, men slew it for the horn, little
caring that their deed removed magic from the world.

rying poles, the women marched a mile to a stream near the pine woods at the far edge of the fields. Its flow barely sufficed for their needs, but they expected the autumn rains to remedy that.

The rains did not come. Each day dawned clear and cloudless; each day the little stream dwindled. At length, the women were forced to return to the wells for their water. They strained the water to take away the evil taste. Nonetheless, it brought disease at once. Those who drank it were seized with cramp and bloody flux, and they communicated the contagion to their comrades. The children suffered most. Large-eyed and dry-lipped, they shrank and withered, and one by one, wailing for water, they began to die.

After several days had come and gone with no abatement of illness, the few villagers who remained healthy gathered in the hut of one of their old women to find the cause of the visitation of death. If it continued, none of them would be alive when the snows came.

The result of this meeting was a curious one to outside eyes, but not, perhaps, to these people. The village elected to offer a sacrifice to propitiate whatever forest witch or demon haunted them. They chose a young woman for the role. She was both fatherless and husbandless, and she had no children. Thus there would be no one to mourn her.

At dusk on the following day, armed with pitchforks and brooms and poles, shouting rhymes and incantations, they drove the young woman from the village, through the parched fields and toward the lowering pines.

She went with what dignity she could muster, neither crying nor running from them. When she reached the verge of the forest, she stopped and held up her hands. So calmly and gravely did she gesture that her neighbors fell silent.

"I go willingly, that the children might live," she said, and then she turned and vanished among the trees. The people of the village made their way home, and none of them looked back.

As for the woman, she walked steadily among the trees, hands folded into her sleeves, head bowed. Night closed in around her. She heard rustlings and murmurings among the pines, and sometimes her skirt was brushed by a scuttling thing, but no demon danced before her and no hand reached out to snatch and claw.

The moon rose and began its journey across the sky. Still, the woman walked on, eyes down, resigned to whatever violent fate awaited her. Suddenly the forest gloom seemed to lighten. When she looked up, a unicorn stood before her, shining, dark-eyed. She knew what it was: Even in her remote village, people had heard tales of unicorns. The woman sank to her knees, and the great beast knelt before her and laid its head against her skirt.

They remained thus for a long time, while the moon set and the stars winked out. At last, when the night faded from black to gray, the maiden rose and placed her hand upon the unicorn's warm withers. It rose and walked beside her.

Straight and proud as a queen, she left the forest and crossed the fields and walked along the village street. Doors swung open at her passing; heads peered from windows. All her neighbors gaped at her—seemingly returned from the dead, and with a royal beast beside her, answering to the pressure of her hand.

And then the unlikely pair went to one well and then the other. At each, the unicorn bowed its head so that the shaft of ivory pierced the surface of the water. When the horn touched it, the water trembled, the slime on its surface dissolved, and it shimmered pure as crystal, clean as sunlight.

The villagers gathered around the maiden and the unicorn. Hesitantly, they stroked its satin sides. It did not flinch at the rough hands. But it daintily stepped sideways to be closer to the woman.

Then a man's voice broke the silence. "Look to the horn," he said sharply. The villagers looked and knew the treasure they had found, and all thought of the magical loveliness of the beast left them. They shoved the woman aside and held her. With pikes and staves they fell upon the unicorn; with furious thrusts they cut it to the heart. And before the light had faded from the dying animal's eyes, they sawed off the precious horn.

It was a long and bloody business, but it was done at last. Then the men of the village skinned the beast—having heard that the skin could be sold as a protection against pests—and butchered it, in case the flesh, too, had value. They hid the horn in wrappings of wool; they loaded the dripping meat into a wooden cart. And two of them set out that afternoon on the track that led to the outside world, intending to sell the harvest of their butchery to the highest bidder.

The story does not tell what became of the woman, or even whether the village prospered. Some accounts say that the villagers traveled south to Istanbul, where they bartered the horn for gold, and the gold for the wonderful goods of the traders who passed through that region—oranges and lemons and pomegranates, fine linens and even bales of silk. These accounts further tell that when the laden carts returned to the village, they bore a hidden cargo—black rats that carried the plague fleas on their bellies. Whether the tales are true is unknown, for no news came from the village. It retreated again into the obscurity that had enfolded it for all the years of its existence.

Yet the villagers' fate hardly mattered. What mattered was their crime, their perfidy in destroying the enchanted beast that had saved them. It had happened often before, of course, but possibly it never happened again. For unicorns seemed to vanish after that. If any had survived mortal hunters, they all fled into their own world, where men could not find them.

Humankind was left with no more than a memory and with relics—rich cups of horn adorned with gold and precious jewels, some small carvings and paintings on manuscripts. And most moving of all were the tapestries that weavers made to record the stories told of the valor and beauty of the unicorn—among all beasts of the elder world, the first in power and beauty and grace.

A Peerless Mount for World-Conquering Alexander

Medieval poets sang of Alexander, the Macedonian King whose armies swept across the world, the man who wept when there were no more lands to conquer. Where Alexander marched, he found wonders, but the greatest was the first—his own mount.

The storytellers said this steed was a mighty horse that bore the proud ivory horn of the unicorn and the emerald-flecked tail of a peacock. It had been the gift of the Queen of Egypt on the

occasion of Alexander's birth, but during his boyhood, it remained unmastered. The great beast could scent the fears of mortals who approached, and it was invincible against them. Only Alexander was devoid of mortal fear, and when he became a man, he sought out the animal. It bowed before him, touching its horn to the dust in token of submission. Alexander accepted its speechless fealty and named the steed Bucephalus, or "oxenheaded," in honor of its enduring strength.

Astride the godlike creature, the young man led his Grecian armies west into Illyria and eastward to Thrace, across the Hellespont and then into the vast provinces of the Persian Empire—the greatest dominion of its day. All whom he met, he

conquered — kings, princes, peasants and other, stranger beings.

In the Persian forests, it was said, Alexander and his men were set upon by hideous remnants of an ancient race — a tribe of manlike creatures covered with dark, oily hair, crowned with branching stag horns and armed with stones. Howling and gibbering, these horrors swarmed among the Greeks. In a moment, the field was a maelstrom of rearing, panicked horses and unnerved men. The army fell back in disarray. But from the disor-

der, one mount charged—Bucephalus the brave, with Alexander shouting the battle paean in a great voice.

In among the wild men he galloped, and behind came his warriors, their courage restored, their swords whistling in the air. Alexander thrust left and right, then leaned from the saddle and, with one hand, grasped the antler of a beast-man. With a sudden twist, he wrenched the horn from its head. The creature stumbled, blood welling from the horn socket and pouring into

its eyes. It issued a long, nightmarish wail, and at the sound, its companions froze and fell silent. Then, darting and twisting among the hoofs of the horses, the beast band fled into its forest, leaving the land to Alexander and his human company.

Alike in valor, the King and his steed sped on into Persia's eastern kingdoms. To Grecian eyes, these were places new and strange, inhabited by creatures few had dreamed of. Alexander slew the powerful among them and set his own rule over the weakened survivors. It was said that he swept over armies made up of warriors that had human bodies and fire-breathing horses'

heads, over races of one-eyed giants; it was said that he fought with dragons. And it was said, most sadly, that he fought even the cousins of Bucephalus.

This happened on the Red Sea shore one night when dusk fell and the Macedonian host prepared to camp. Before the tents were fully pitched, however, a high, familiar call echoed amid the gathering shadows. It was a summons to Bucephalus, but the great beast did not answer. Nor did Bucephalus appear when a unicorn tribe—fierce, wild and free—thundered toward the encampment. The unicorns' hoofs sent tremors through the earth,

and their massive heads were lowered, aligning their horns to kill
the mortals who had invaded their territory. But nothing could
daunt Alexander's warriors now. One and all, the unicorns died,
their hearts split by Grecian lances, their blood spilled out by
the bitter edges of Grecian swords. Bucephalus never joined
them: His loyalty was no longer to his own kind. It had been
given to Alexander the Conqueror, greatest among men.

All the earth was the Macedonian's to command, it seemed.
Then he sought, some chroniclers said, to subjugate the heavens. In a chariot pulled by captured griffins—those winged lions

of India and Persia—Alexander sailed one day into the sky.
Below him, small as toys, were the tents of his vast encampment;
minute as flowers were the trees that studded the plain. He urged
the winged beasts higher, until the sea beside the plain was no
more than a sheet of gold. Then he turned his face upward,
directly toward the sun.

But when he faced the steady eye of heaven and met with his
own eye the power of that eternal lamp, Alexander retreated, no
god but only a man. He brought the griffins down to earth and
captivity, and he assailed the skies no more. For the rest of his

life, Alexander trod the earth like other men. And mighty
though he was, he had no answer to death. Bucephalus' great
heart failed at last. The valiant beast died, and Alexander
grieved; it was said that he built a city in the unicorn's honor.
    Alexander himself died soon after, only three years past his

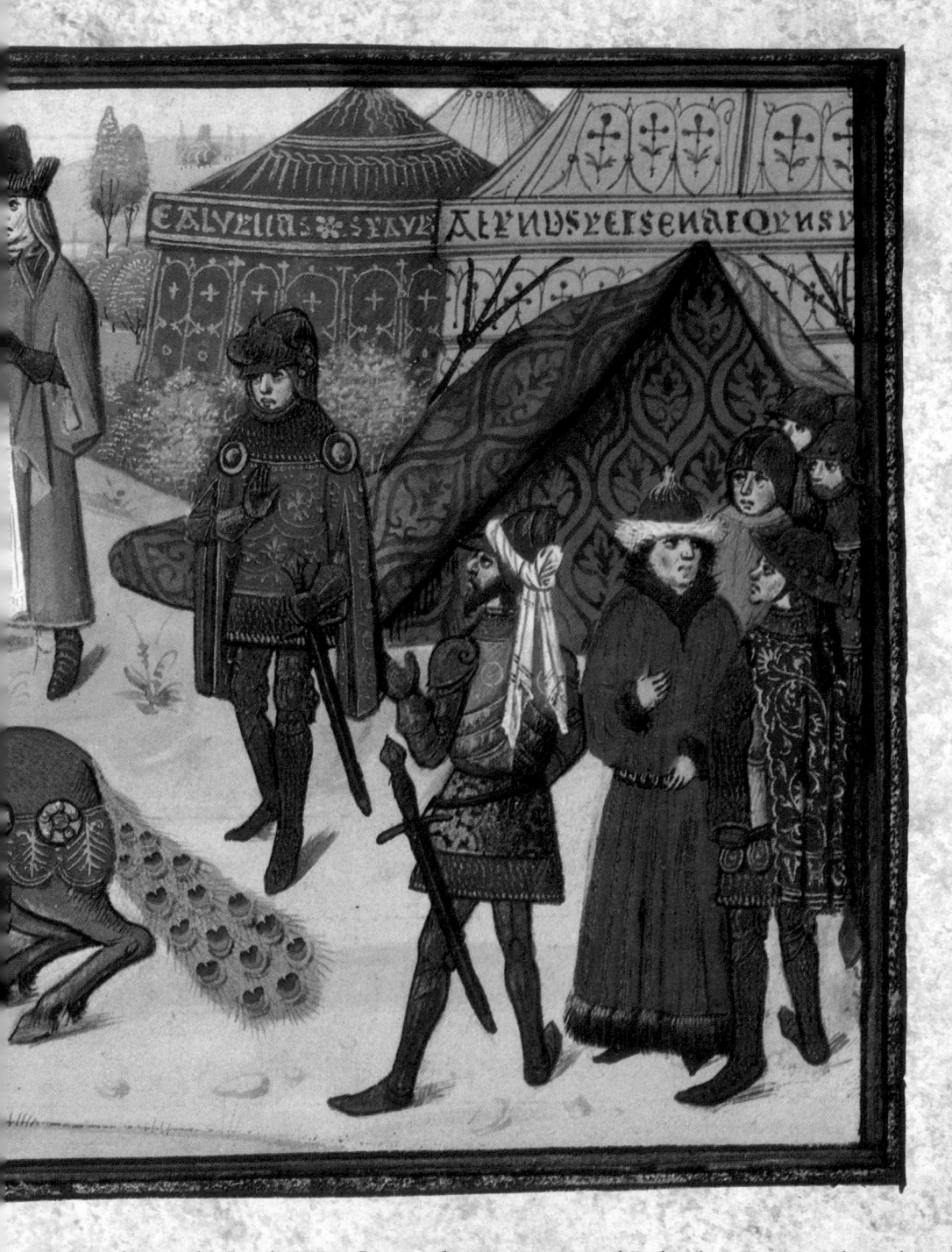

thirtieth birthday. Soon the territories he had conquered and forged into a single great empire again split apart. In time, cities he had built crumbled and fell. Few signs of his power remained—only tumbled stones, the scattered bones of his armies, and the glittering dust of the unicorn's horn.

Acknowledgments

The editors are particularly indebted to John Dorst, consultant, for his help in the preparation of this volume. The editors also wish to thank the following persons and institutions: Rolf Andrée, Kunstmuseum, Düsseldorf; François Avril, Curator, Département des Manuscrits, Bibliothèque Nationale, Paris; Milo C. Beach, Curator of Indian Art, Freer Gallery of Art, Smithsonian Institution, Washington, D.C.; Biblioteca Casanatense, Rome; Yu-ying Brown, Department of Oriental Manuscripts and Printed Books, British Library, London; John Carlson, Center for Archeo-Astronomy, University of Maryland, College Park, Maryland; Giancarlo Costa, Milan; Sophie De Bussière, Curator, Musée du Petit-Palais, Paris; Marie-Henriette De Pommerol, Paris; Martin Forrest, Bourne Fine Art Ltd., Edinburgh; Jacqueline L. Fowler, Stamford, Connecticut; Kenneth Gardner, Deputy Keeper, Department of Oriental Manuscripts and Printed Books, British Library, London; Marielise Göpel, Archiv für Kunst und Geschichte, West Berlin; Klauss Hess, Registrar, Öffentliche Kunstsammlung, Kunstmuseum, Basel, Switzerland; Christine Hofmann, Bayerische Staatsgemäldesammlungen, Munich; Joan Hornby, Nationalmuseets Etnografiske Samling, Copenhagen; Ann Hughey, Potomac, Maryland; G. Irvine, Department of Oriental Antiquities, British Museum, London; Heidi Klein, Bildarchiv Preussischer Kulturbesitz, West Berlin; Shigeru Koide, Kirin Brewing Company Ltd., Tokyo; Bernd Krimmel, Director, Institut Mathildenhöhe, Darmstadt; J. P. Losty, Assistant Keeper, Department of Oriental Manuscripts and Printed Books, British Library, London; Heinrich Lützeler, Kunsthistorisches Institut, Bonn; Beth McInlock, Department of Oriental Manuscripts and Printed Books, British Library, London; Gabriele Mandel, Milan; Heinz Mode, Halle, East Germany; Beatrice Premoli, Museo Nazionale delle Arti e Tradizioni Popolari, Rome; Walt Reed, Illustration House, South Norwalk, Connecticut; Jo Ann Reisler, Vienna, Virginia; Luisa Ricciarini, Milan; Lores Riva, Milan; B. W. Robinson, London; Scala, Florence; Justin Schiller, New York City; Lawrence Seeborg, Greenbelt, Maryland; Mitsuhiko Shibata, Atomi University, Tokyo; Marie Lukens Swietochowski, Associate Curator, Islamic Division, Metropolitan Museum of Art, New York City; Verity Wilson, Far Eastern Section, Victoria and Albert Museum, London; Clara Young, Keeper of Art, Dundee Art Gallery, Scotland.

Bibliography

Aryan, K. C., and Subhashini Aryan, *Hanumān in Art and Mythology*. Delhi, India: Rekha Prakashan, 1976.

Ashton, John, *Curious Creatures in Zoology*. Detroit: Singing Tree Press, 1968 (reprint of 1890 edition).

Barber, Richard, and Anne Riches, *A Dictionary of Fabulous Beasts*. London: Macmillan, 1971.

Barry, Mary Elizabeth, and Paul R. Hanna, *Wonder Flights of Long Ago*. New York: D. Appleton and Co., 1930.*

Beach, Milo Cleveland, *The Adventures of Rama*. Washington, D.C.: Freer Gallery of Art, Smithsonian Institution, 1983.*

Borges, Jorge Luis, with Margarita Guerrero, *The Book of Imaginary Beings*. Transl. by Norman Thomas di Giovanni. New York: E. P. Dutton, 1969.*

Brusewitz, Gunnar, *Hunting*. Transl. by Walstan Wheeler. New York: Stein and Day, 1969.

Bulfinch, Thomas, *Myths of Greece and Rome*. Comp. by Bryan Holme. New York: Penguin Books, 1981.*

Campbell, Joseph:
The Masks of God: Occidental Mythology. New York: Penguin Books, 1980.
The Way of the Animals Powers. Vol. 1 of *Historical Atlas of World Mythology*. New York: Alfred van der Marck, 1983.

Child, Francis James, ed., *The English and Scottish Popular Ballads*. Vol. 1. Boston: Houghton Mifflin, 1883.

Chorlton, Windsor, *Ice Ages* (Planet Earth series). Alexandria, Virginia: Time-Life Books, 1983.

Clair, Colin, *Unnatural History: An Illustrated Bestiary*. New York: Abelard-Schuman, 1967.

Clark, R. T. Rundle, *Myth and Symbol in Ancient Egypt*. London: Thames and Hudson, 1978.*

Costello, Peter, *The Magic Zoo: The Natural History of Fabulous Animals*. New York: St. Martin's Press, 1979.*

Cottrell, Leonard, *The Bull of Minos*. New York: Rinehart, 1959.

Dowson, John, *A Classical Dictionary of Hindu Mythology and Religion, Geography, History, and Literature*. London: Trübner & Co., 1879.

Dulac, Edmund, *Edmund Dulac's Picture Book for the American Red Cross*. London: Hodder and Stoughton for *The Daily Telegraph*, circa 1916.

Edey, Maitland, *Lost World of the Aegean* (The Emergence of Man series). New York: Time-Life Books, 1975.

Egyptian Mythology. New York: Tudor Publishing, 1965.

Ettinghausen, Richard, *The Unicorn*. Vol. 1 of *Studies in Muslim Iconography*. Washington, D.C.: Freer Gallery of Art, Smithsonian Institution, 1950.*

Euripides, *The Bacchae. Hippolytus. Alcestis. Medea* (The Laurel Classical Drama). Ed. by Robert W. Corrigan. New York: Dell, 1973 (reprint).

Ferguson, John C., and Masaharu Anesaki, *Chinese, Japanese*. Vol. 8 of *The Mythology of All Races*. Boston: Marshall Jones, 1928.

Fermor, Patrick Leigh, *Roumeli. Travels in Northern Greece*. New York: Penguin Books, 1983.

Firdausí, *The Sháh Námeh*. Transl. by James Atkinson. London: Printed for the Oriental Translation Fund of Great Britain and Ireland, 1832.

Freeman, Margaret B., *The Unicorn Tapestries*. New York: E. P. Dutton (for The Metropolitan Museum of Art), 1983.*

Gallant, Roy A., *The Constellations: How They Came to Be*. New York: Four Winds Press, 1979.

Gould, Charles, *Mythical Monsters*. Detroit: Singing Tree Press, 1969 (reprint of 1886 edition).

Graves, Robert, *The Greek Myths*. Vols. 1 and 2. New York: Penguin Books, 1983.*

Gregory, Lady, ed. and transl., *Gods and Fighting Men: The Story of the Tuatha De Danaan and of the Fianna of Ireland*. Gerrards Cross, England: Colin Smythe, 1979 (reprint of 1904 edition).*

Hathaway, Nancy, *The Unicorn*. New York: Viking Press, 1980.

Howey, M. Oldfield, *The Horse in Magic and Myth*. London: William Rider & Son, 1923.

Joly, Henri L., *Legend in Japanese Art*.

Rutland, Vermont: Charles E. Tuttle, 1967.

Jones, Gwyn, and Thomas Jones, transls., *The Mabinogion*. Hendrik-Ido-Ambacht, The Netherlands: Dragon's Dream B.V., 1982.

Kaye, Sidney, *Handbook of Emergency Toxicology: A Guide for the Identification, Diagnosis, and Treatment of Poisoning*. Springfield, Illinois: Charles C. Thomas, 1980.

Keith, A. Berriedale, and Albert J. Carnoy, *Indian, Iranian*. Vol. 6 of *The Mythology of All Races*. Boston: Marshall Jones, 1917.

Komroff, Manuel, ed., *The Travels of Marco Polo (The Venetian)*. New York: Liveright, 1982.

Leach, Maria, ed., *Funk & Wagnalls Standard Dictionary of Folklore, Mythology and Legend*. 2 vols. New York: Funk & Wagnalls, 1949.*

"Le Livre des Merveilles." Unpublished ms. Paris: Bibliothèque Nationale, circa 1410.

Locket, S., with W.S.M. Grieve and S. G. Harrison, *Clinical Toxicology: The Clinical Diagnosis and Treatment of Poisoning*. London: Henry Kimpton, 1957.

Lum, Peter, *Fabulous Beasts*. London: Thames and Hudson, 1952.

MacManus, Seumas, *The Story of the Irish Race. A Popular History of Ireland*. Old Greenwich, Connecticut: The Devin-Adair Co., 1983 (revision of 1921 edition).

Manning-Sanders, Ruth, ed., *A Book of Magical Beasts*. Camden, New Jersey: Thomas Nelson, 1970.

McCullough, Helen Craig, transl., *Yoshitsune: A Fifteenth-Century Japanese Chronicle*. Stanford, California: Stanford University Press, 1966.

Mertz, Barbara, *Red Land, Black Land: Daily Life in Ancient Egypt*. New York: Dodd, Mead, 1978.

Moeschlin, Sven, *Poisoning: Diagnosis and Treatment*. Transl. by Jenifer Bickel. New York: Grune & Stratton, 1965.

Nott, Stanley Charles, ed., *Chinese Culture in the Arts*. New York: Chinese Culture Study Group of America, 1946.

Owen, The Reverend Elias, *Welsh Folk-Lore*. Norwood, Pennsylvania: Norwood Editions, 1973 (reprint of 1896 edition).

Perry, Frances, *Flowers of the World*. London: Hamlyn, 1972.

Rees, Alwyn, and Brinley Rees, *Celtic Heritage: Ancient Tradition in Ireland and Wales*. London: Thames and Hudson, 1961.*

Robin, P. Ansell, *Animal Lore in English Literature*. Darby, Pennsylvania: The Folcroft Press, 1970 (reprint of 1932 edition).

Ross, Anne, *Pagan Celtic Britain: Studies in Iconography and Tradition*. London: Routledge and Kegan Paul, 1967.*

Shepard, Odell, *The Lore of the Unicorn*. New York: Avenel Books, 1982 (reprint of 1930 edition).*

Silverberg, Barbara, ed., *Phoenix Feathers: A Collection of Mythical Monsters*. New York: E. P. Dutton, no date.

Spence, Lewis, *Myths & Legends of Ancient Egypt*. London: George G. Harrap, 1949 (reprint of 1915 edition).*

"Tengu no Dairi." ("The Palace of the Tengu.") Unpublished ms. London: British Library, early 17th Century.

Thompson, C.J.S., *Poisons and Poisoners*. London: Harold Shaylor, 1931.

Thubron, Colin, *The Ancient Mariners* (The Seafarers series). Alexandria, Virginia: Time-Life Books, 1981.

Topsell, Edward, *Topsell's Histories of Beasts*. Ed. by Malcolm South. Chicago: Nelson-Hall, 1981.

The Travels of Sir John Mandeville. The Journal of Friar Odoric. London: J. M. Dent & Sons, 1928.

Vinycomb, John, *Fictitious & Symbolic Creatures in Art. With Special Reference to Their Use in British Heraldry*.

Detroit: Gale Research, 1969 (reprint of 1906 edition).

Volker, T., *The Animal in Far Eastern Art*. Leiden, The Netherlands: E. J. Brill, 1950.

Warner, Rex, *The Stories of the Greeks*. New York: Farrar, Straus & Giroux, 1967.

Watson, Jane Werner, ed., *Rama of the Golden Age*. Champaign, Illinois: Garrard Publishing, 1971.

Wauquelin, Jean, "L'Histoire du Roi Alexandre." Unpublished ms. Paris: Ville de Paris-Musée du Petit Palais, mid-15th Century.

Wittkower, Rudolf, *Allegory and the Migration of Symbols*. Boulder, Colorado: Westview Press, 1977.*

Wyatt, Stanley P., *Principles of Astronomy*. Boston: Allyn and Bacon, 1974.

Titles marked with an asterisk were especially helpful in the preparation of this volume.

Picture Credits

TIME-LIFE BOOKS

EUROPEAN EDITOR: Kit van Tulleken
Assistant European Editor: Gillian Moore
Design Director: Ed Skyner
Photography Director: Pamela Marke
Chief of Research: Vanessa Kramer
Chief Sub-Editor: Ilse Gray

THE ENCHANTED WORLD

SERIES DIRECTOR: Ellen Phillips
Deputy Editor: Robin Richman
Designer: Dale Pollekoff
Series Administrator: Jane Edwin

Editorial Staff for *Magical Beasts*
Staff Writer: Daniel Stashower
Researchers: Janet Doughty, Myrna E. Traylor
(principals), Linda Lee,
Patricia N. McKinney
Assistant Designer: Lorraine D. Rivard
Copy Coordinator: Barbara Fairchild Quarmby
Picture Coordinator: Nancy C. Scott
Editorial Assistant: Constance B. Strawbridge

Special Contributor: Jennifer B. Gilman

Correspondents: Elisabeth Kraemer-Singh
(Bonn); Margot Hapgood, Dorothy Bacon
(London); Miriam Hsia (New York);
Maria Vincenza Aloisi, Josephine du Brusle
(Paris); Ann Natanson (Rome). Valuable
assistance was also provided by:
Ardis Grosjean, Lois Lorimer, Anita Rich
(Copenhagen); Felix Rosenthal (Moscow);
Carolyn Chubert, Christina Lieberman
(New York); Dick Berry (Tokyo).

Editorial Production
Chief: Jane Hawker
Art Department: Helen Jones
Production Assistants: Alan Godwin,
Maureen Kelly
Editorial Department: Theresa John,
Debra Lelliott

ISBN 7054 0886 8

TIME-LIFE is a trademark of Time
Incorporated U.S.A.

Chief Series Consultant

Tristram Potter Coffin, Professor of
English at the University of Pennsylvania,
is a leading authority on folklore. He is the
author or editor of numerous books and
more than 100 articles. His best-known
works are *The British Traditional Ballad in
North America, The Old Ball Game, The Book of
Christmas Folklore* and *The Female Hero*.

This volume is one of a series that is based
on myths, legends and folk tales.

TIME
LIFE
BOOKS

THE ENCHANTED WORLD
LIBRARY OF NATIONS
HOME REPAIR AND IMPROVEMENT
CLASSICS OF EXPLORATION
PLANET EARTH
PEOPLES OF THE WILD
THE EPIC OF FLIGHT
THE SEAFARERS
WORLD WAR II
THE GOOD COOK
THE TIME-LIFE ENCYCLOPAEDIA OF GARDENING
THE GREAT CITIES
THE OLD WEST
THE WORLD'S WILD PLACES
THE EMERGENCE OF MAN
LIFE LIBRARY OF PHOTOGRAPHY
TIME-LIFE LIBRARY OF ART
GREAT AGES OF MAN
LIFE SCIENCE LIBRARY
LIFE NATURE LIBRARY
THE TIME-LIFE BOOK OF BOATING
TECHNIQUES OF PHOTOGRAPHY
LIFE AT WAR
LIFE GOES TO THE MOVIES
BEST OF LIFE
LIFE IN SPACE

PRINTED AND BOUND BY BREPOLS S.A.-TURNHOUT, BELGIUM

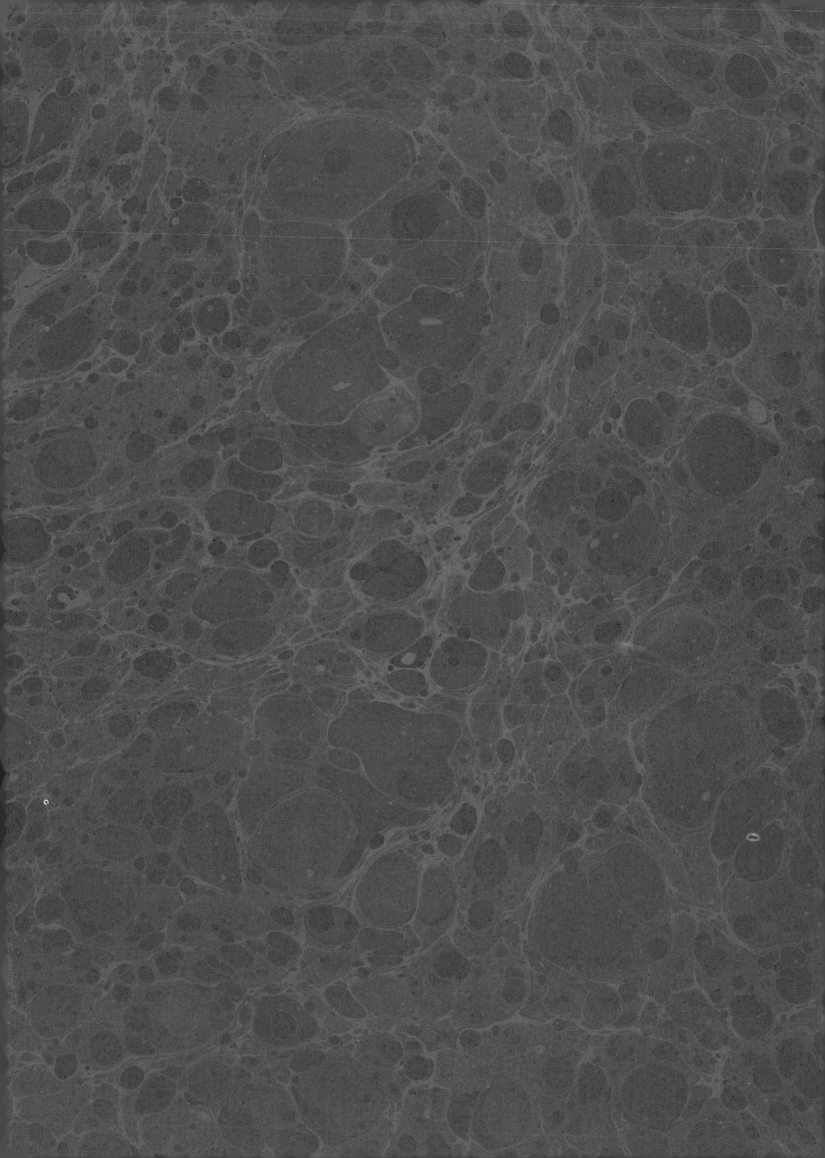